Precipice

Beth Dana Kemp

For my mother

Prologue

Everything is heavy—his body and his mind. The sound of waves crashing upon a distant shore echoes in his ears. He is reluctant to abandon his cocoon of safety and squeezes his eyes shut in an effort to remain blind to IT, but some compelling force—Truth— grabs his elbow and pulls him across the threshold into consciousness. His arms and legs are deadweight and slow to respond to his brain's commands as though they, too, fear what is approaching. It is an effort to open his eyes, and when he finally does, everything is hazy. A thick fog moves past him sluggishly, its cold fingers trailing a thin layer of moisture on his skin. Something hard and unyielding bites at his shoulder blade. *Where am I?* he thinks. His head lolls listlessly to the left where a muted, yellow light peers back at him through a backdrop of gray. As the light gets brighter, the sound of rolling waves fades away until he's enveloped in a foreboding, deathlike silence.

A cool breeze skips over his damp skin, and goose bumps rise, mocking his weakness. A shiver passes through him, and accompanying it, is clarity. The mist has lifted, and his vision is crisp, no longer gauzy around the edges. He realizes that he is standing and leaning against an open doorway. Soundlessly, he shifts his position and automatically rubs at the pins and needles sensation in his shoulder.

He sees the boy sitting on a hastily-made bed. Two large pillows prop up his small body as he slowly turns the glossy pages of a comic book. Absently, he swipes at the light brown hair that hangs over his eyes. His lips move as he reads, his small finger keeping pace with the words. He is wearing a Spiderman tee-shirt and a pair of black shorts. The boy doesn't notice him standing there, watching.

There is something familiar about the boy. He sees himself in him. He shifts uncomfortably, scuffing the floor, and the boy's head whips up, but he's not looking at him. He's gazing intently through the open door, his head cocked at an uncomfortable angle. He watches as the boy scrambles from the bed, the comic book falling, forgotten, to the floor.

A blast of searing heat ricochets throughout his body as the boy passes by him. The man rocks back on his heels from the intensity and reaches blindly for the doorjamb to keep himself upright. With the heat, comes a volley of sound, obliterating the earlier silence with a ferocious energy. Enraged shouts, desperate pleas, terrified screams, and the sound of shattering glass assault his ears. Each sound causes him to cringe and shrink back in horror. He covers his ears with his hands, pushing as hard as he can, willing the sounds to stop. Panic races through his body, the urge to flee is palpable, but, instead, he turns toward the sound and takes a step.

The boy is standing on the first stair, his hands attempting to smother his own ears as rivers of tears stain his face. The boy turns toward him, his eyes turbulent, silently begging him to do

5

something, but the man is frozen in place. The boy turns away, disappointed, and darts into a nearby room.

The man is alone now. Unnatural moans drift up the stairs, causing the fine hairs on the back of his neck to stand. He feels a teardrop roll across his cheek and begin its descent down his face. He swipes at it, confused, unaware that he'd been crying. When he looks at his hand, a smear of blood mars the smooth pink of his palm. He frantically wipes at his face, but there is an ocean of blood. His shirt is painted with blackish-red spatter.

His breath hitches and a scream climbs up his throat, but it is choked by fear. Only long, heavy gasps emerge from his lips. Without warning, his feet bring him to the top of the stairs; he is now standing in the place the boy just vacated. His toes curl helplessly over the lip of the first stair, unwilling to take that first step. He hovers at this precipice, loath to confront the monster within the house.

He closes his eyes tightly. He is reluctant to see the evil that summons him, but then he hears IT. Low, guttural whispers float up the stairs. He can feel them reverberating in his own throat, reaching for him, beckoning him to come closer. The boy is shouting at him, but he can't make out his words. He opens his eyes and, mesmerized, starts down the stairs. At the bottom, he obediently turns to the left and finds himself standing before a red door. He is near the monster; he can smell IT—a horrible coppery scent that reminds him of raw meat. Blood seeps from beneath the door, soaking the beige carpeting in the hallway, but he stares, transfixed.

The pool of gore creeps closer and closer to his bare feet. He cannot turn away. Instead, he walks submissively toward the scarlet door, hand in hand with IT.

CHAPTER 1

Jake sat in biology impatiently waiting for the three o'clock bell to signal his freedom from the constraints of school. Even though he was a good student, he couldn't wait for this particular school day to end. He willed the clock's minute hand to move faster, but it seemed like three minutes passed before it finally hopped forward with a loud click. Jake picked up his pencil and began doodling. Time always seemed to move in slow motion when he was looking forward to something. He and his two best friends, Ryan and Adam, were planning to go to High Falls Gorge to swim and, Jake was hoping, to hang out with Amber Green, the blue-eyed beauty who sat next to him in English.

Jake looked over at Ryan who sat across the classroom, half-reclined in his seat and wearing his signature "I don't give a shit" expression that he saved especially for Mrs. Drake's biology class. His long legs were splayed, one beneath his desk and the other barricading the aisle. Ryan glanced at Jake, looked pointedly at his watch and tapped it a few times. Jake rolled his eyes in return; it was like time had come to a standstill.

The two had become friends when Jake moved to Brushton to live with his grandparents ten years ago. Back then, they'd shared a passion for baseball, fishing, exploring the woods behind Ryan's house, and hating girls. Now, Ryan hated biology and was barely passing, and they had both, long ago, decided to give girls another chance.

At seventeen, they seemed, to their classmates and teachers, like polar opposites. Jake excelled in school; Ryan hated everything about it. Jake was quiet, polite, and mild-mannered; Ryan was arrogant, rude, and sarcastic, but Jake knew, *really knew*, that he could rely on Ryan for anything.

Jake glanced at the clock once again—only ten more minutes remained until they could begin enjoying their weekend. There would only be a few more opportunities to head to the gorge before the weather turned too cold. Already it was mid-October, but it was unseasonably warm for upstate New York. This could be Jake's last chance to be alone with Amber, and he had something to ask her.

Jake allowed his mind to rewind three months to the day they'd met. He'd been with Adam, his other best friend, that day. It was July, and the sun's blazing heat had forced many to gather at the small lake beneath the falls at the gorge. Usually, Ryan, Adam, and Jake would go swimming together, but Ryan was at a local college attending basketball camp.

"I'm glad Ryan's at camp," Adam said as the boys descended the rocky trail that led to the pool. "Maybe *we'll* finally get a chance to talk to some girls."

There was actually a lot of truth in Adam's statement. Girls seemed to flock to Ryan. He was tall, handsome, stylish, and had an air of supreme confidence. If flirting were a class in school, Ryan would be teaching it. Unfortunately, Adam would be immediately enrolled in the remedial class with summer school in his future. Jake playfully shoved Adam away. "You'd have a much better chance if you'd stop using such stupid pickup lines. What was the one you used on Jodi the other day?" Jake teased. "Oh wait…I remember." He cleared his throat and continued dramatically, "You must be the reason for global warming because *you* are so hot."

Adam grinned. "I thought that was a good one. It *did* make her smile."

Jake snorted. "Everyone was smiling. You said it in McDonalds…in line…during the lunch rush…and very loudly I might add! You sounded like a stalker. I'm surprised she didn't kick you in the nut sack and run away."

"What can I say?" Adam replied matter-of-factly, shrugging his shoulders. "I'm just a hopeless romantic."

"You're hopeless all right," Jake quipped.

As they turned the last corner and emerged from the trees, a chaotic scene met them. Children of all ages splashed and shouted, their shrieks of delight rising over the roar of the waterfall. A cluster of mothers sat together on lawn chairs to keep an eye on their children while enjoying some adult conversation. The view always amazed Jake, and he paused to soak it in. Giant, flat rocks broke the surface of the water. This geologic wonder created a ring of small islands near the shoreline and provided teens with semi-seclusion for sunbathing, reading, playing cards, or talking. Jake's friends usually commandeered the two rocks furthest away from the screaming kids. Jake heard a loud shout and, shielding his eyes against the sun, looked up at the footbridge that spanned the gorge near the top of the waterfall. There were a few teenagers on the bridge enjoying the cool mist coming from the falls. They waved and Jake waved back.

As the two boys wove through the crowd, Jake saw her. Amber was absolutely stunning, filling out her bikini quite nicely, he'd noted. She was sunbathing, and her long, tan legs contrasted nicely with her white beach towel. "Who's that?" he whispered to Adam.

"Who?" Adam asked obliviously. He'd set his sights on Jodi who sat with a few of her friends. He reluctantly tore his eyes away and followed Jake's gaze. "Whoa. I have no idea, but she's a goddess," Adam responded, staring intently. "She's a definite ten."

Jake nudged his friend whose intense stare bordered on 'psychotic molester.' Adam was anything but subtle. Jake playfully slapped the back of Adam's head. "You should probably consider wiping away that drool if you're planning on talking to her," he joked.

Only then did Adam come out of his love struck reverie, shaking his head as though coming out of a dream. He wiped his hand across his mouth dramatically, making unpleasant slurping noises. He gestured grandly at the crowd. "We're surrounded by girls in bikinis and you think a little slobber is uncalled for?" he asked a little too loudly.

A few girls rolled their eyes at Adam, so Jake led him away before he could make an even greater fool of himself. Adam allowed himself to be guided but continued to look around, appreciating the view.

As the two continued walking toward their group of friends, Jake's gaze returned to the girl who was now lying on her back reading a book. He just couldn't stop staring at her. Adam was right; there were a lot of girls around, but Jake was drawn to this particular girl. "It's a good thing Ryan isn't here. He'd already be hitting on her, and he always gets the girl."

Adam laughed mockingly. "I don't think even *he'd* be able to pick up this one. She'd probably laugh in his face. She's, like, model-hot! C'mon, let's go talk to her," Adam said impatiently. Adam was never nervous to start a conversation with a girl, and that was probably his biggest problem.

Jake quickly sidestepped in front of Adam, effectively blocking his view of the beautiful stranger and forcing him to meet his very serious gaze. "No pickup lines," Jake warned. "I will piss-pound you if you embarrass me. Got it?"

"You suck, Jake. I had the perfect one picked out too. Wanna hear it?" he asked hopefully.

"No," Jake stated simply but firmly as he turned abruptly away.

When the two boys had introduced themselves to Amber, she had surprised both of them. They had expected a snob, someone who thought she was too good to speak to them, but she was fantastic. She was the prettiest girl Jake had ever seen. Her smile was incredible, her teeth white and even. Her blond hair was pulled back into a ponytail, and when she took off her sunglasses, her eyes were bright blue. She had recently moved to the area from Syracuse with her family. She had two younger sisters and a dog, and her parents were actually still married...to each other. Jake had fallen for her right away...and so had Adam.

"I can't believe how cool she is," Adam told Ryan later that evening. He counted off each of Amber's attributes on his fingers as he spoke. "One—her dad used to be the assistant basketball coach at Syracuse University, so Amber actually likes watching ESPN. Two—she plays basketball and volleyball, and she even likes to golf and bowl. Three—she's wicked funny and four—she out-burped me in a contest. I'm telling you, Ryan, she's perfect."

Ryan feigned a yawn. "Blah, blah, blah...how are her tits, Adam? That's the real question."

Adam gasped, "How dare you objectify my future wife like that, you peckerhead? That's just not cool, man." A smile spread across his face as he visualized the perky breasts barely contained within the bikini top. "I will say, though, that they are. Pretty. Fucking. Awesome...just sayin'."

"I second that," Jake added.

Adam leaned back on the couch and placed his feet on the coffee table. "That's right, boys," he declared cockily, "some day that hot little number will be my wife. She'll be proud to call herself Mrs. Adam Krovlovski."

Ryan rolled his eyes and threw a handful of popcorn at Adam. "Get real...as if she'd marry you, you idiot. Just wait until she gets a look at my goods." He flexed his muscles and kissed each bicep.

"She won't even remember your names," Ryan added casually, dismissing both Adam and Jake with a wave of his hand.

*   *   *

When Jake looked up at the clock, he saw that only five minutes had gone by. *Why does this class drag by so slowly?* He figured it had something to do with Mrs. Drake's monotonous voice. It had an almost hypnotizing effect. At the moment she was rambling on and on about genetics. A quick peek around the classroom only confirmed his belief that his biology teacher was the epitome of boredom. His classmates' eyes were either at half-mast, glazed over, or actually closed. Jake promised himself that he would read the chapter in his textbook during the weekend so he could continue his daydream about Amber.

It had been hilarious when Ryan met Amber three days later. They were at the gorge once again. He'd been strutting around and flexing his muscles (he thought inconspicuously). He'd never had any problem attracting girls. At six feet, two inches in height with a body that looked as though it had been sculpted out of granite, most girls found him quite attractive. His brown hair was longish and wavy and had a tendency to fall over his eyes, and his signature hair flip (which looked more like the beginning of a seizure to Jake and Adam) left many girls quaking. Ryan figured he'd have Amber eating out of his hand in no time.

Unfortunately for Ryan, Amber hadn't taken him seriously from the start. In fact, she had teased him so much on that first day that his huge ego threatened to crumble. After that day, Ryan referred to her as "The Dyke," and she referred to him as "Pompous Ass." It was true hate from that point onward. Meanwhile, Jake had fallen even more deeply in love with her. He'd never seen anyone take on Ryan like that and, to be honest, he had enjoyed every bit of it.

It was true that, compared to Ryan, he wasn't much to look at. He was almost as tall as Ryan, but he was thin and lanky. He was very athletic and could run for miles without breaking a sweat. His light brown hair was cut very short, not really the height of fashion, but he couldn't be bothered taking the time to fix his hair in the morning. He knew that Ryan took at least a half hour every morning perfecting his messy-on-purpose look and, to be honest, he really couldn't stand Ryan's constant hair flip. "Someday you're going to paralyze yourself, and someone will have to wipe your ass for you," Jake teased frequently. "Which one of your many girlfriends will do that?"

Suddenly, Jake tuned back in to the blathering Mrs. Drake. She was giving them an assignment on a Friday right before dismissal. *What a witch,* he thought to himself.

As Mrs. Drake spoke, she paced back and forth across the front of the room and fiddled with her whiteboard marker. Her students had dubbed her "the ping pong pacer." Jake watched his now-alert classmates' heads track her progress. They looked as though they were following an intense tennis match. Her brown orthopedic shoes quietly squeaked each time she changed direction.

15

"You'll need to speak extensively with your family to help you with this. This is a major project and will account for 30 percent of this quarter's grade, so I want you to put a lot of time and effort into this. You have two weeks, but I'd start immediately if I were you. I know how many of you like to procrastinate." She glanced over at Ryan and gave him a withering look which said, *I'm talking to you, moron.*

Ryan piped up in a sickeningly sweet tone, "Mrs. Drake, you know how much I love your projects. They're always so much fun and well-thought out. I wouldn't think of procrastinating."

"Ryan, why would I ever accuse you of procrastinating?" she replied just as pleasantly. Jake even thought he'd seen her bat her eyelashes. She started back toward the whiteboard, but spun around. She took two steps toward Ryan's desk and said, with just the right hint of venom, "Oh, I remember. Maybe it's because you haven't turned in a single assignment on time yet this year." Mrs. Drake gave Ryan a dismissive look and turned back to the board.

Jake shook his head and smiled. She may seem old, but she moved like a jungle cat. The rest of the class snickered at Ryan's expense. It certainly wasn't the first time that old lady Drake had gotten the best of Ryan. Most of Drake's students were smart enough not to tangle with her. Although she looked thin and frail, she could really bite back when provoked. Watching her verbally spar with a smartass student was the most exciting thing about her class. It was the only time anyone ever paid attention.

Jake blanched when he looked at the board to copy down the assignment he'd totally ignored. He immediately felt as though he'd been punched in the gut. The board read:

> **Write a family history that extends back three generations. Record facts about your ancestors' childhoods, work histories, personality/physical traits, etc. Try to trace your traits back to your ancestors. Consider the role of genetics in your lives.**

Jake's fingers shook and he dropped his pencil. It rolled, unnoticed, onto the floor. *Oh, my God! What am I going to do? I can't do this assignment? I can't let anyone find out,* thought Jake, silently writhing in his seat. His stomach flip-flopped, and a surge of hatred for Mrs. Drake welled up inside him. A sheen of perspiration appeared above his upper lip. Just then the bell rang, and the happy cheers of his classmates hyped for the weekend punctuated the roar in Jake's ears.

*　　　*　　　*

"There it is, Amber," Sandy sang out excitedly as the car rolled to a stop.

Amber's eyes followed Sandy's pointing finger as she turned off the ignition and unbuckled her seatbelt. Her heart fluttered, and she was instantly filled with nervous energy. The parking area was filled with cars, and, even though she'd expected to see it, she was still thrilled to see Jake's beat-up, rusty pickup truck.

Sandy gathered their towels from the backseat. "I still don't understand why you'd choose Jake over Ryan," she managed to say around a mouthful of gum.

Amber studied her new neighbor, this energetic girl who had torn over on her four-wheeler before the movers had even removed one box from the giant truck parked in the driveway. She put her hands on her hips and said what she always said since the day she first met Ryan. "Ryan Chapin is the biggest a-hole I've ever met, and I've met quite a few people in my short lifetime." She walked around to the trunk and pulled out a small cooler and a red and black checked blanket.

Sandy just giggled in return. She liked teasing Amber about Ryan; it was always so easy to get a rise out of her. "But you have to admit that he is hot. You can't say he isn't," Sandy continued, as she turned to hide her grin.

"His revolting personality makes him quite vomitous," Amber replied in a British accent. She jogged in front of Sandy and spun around, now walking backwards. She wagged her finger in Sandy's face and said authoritatively, "That's the problem with young people today...all you care about is the outside. It's the inside that counts, and Ryan is rotten to the core."

A round pink bubble emerged between Sandy's lips, and Amber pounced, ready to pop it in her face, but Sandy sucked it back in with a smirk before Amber had the chance. "Did you take theater classes in Syracuse?" Sandy asked, chewing loudly.

"Ugh…you chew like a cow. It's so gross," Amber scolded as she held out her hand in front of Sandy's mouth. Without pausing, Sandy spit the offensive gum into the proffered palm. Amber shrieked and flung the gum into a bush before shaking her hand furiously. "Germs…cooties…get them off!"

Amber tried to rub her hand on Sandy's shirt, but she whirled away. Instantly, Amber was quiet once again as though nothing had happened. Sandy looked at her curiously when Amber calmly stated, "Theater? No. Why would you ask if I took theater?" Sandy shoved her away and laughed so hard tears rolled down her cheeks.

Sandy was the first person to welcome the Green family. Amber still had to get used to this new definition of "neighbor." Before she'd moved to this small town, her neighbors lived so close that she'd felt claustrophobic. While Sandy's house was visible from Amber's, it was still about a quarter of a mile away. Even though she was a freshman and two years younger than Amber, they had hit it off immediately, although Sandy's bubbly personality and willingness to help unpack certainly helped. She was also really good with Amber's younger sisters who were eight and ten and readily offered up her babysitting services which, thankfully, had given Amber time to make new friends.

The girls carefully made their way up the trail that wound from the parking lot to the top of the gorge. The other trail led down to the small lake, but Jake had told her to meet him at the waterfall. Sandy had been the first person to tell her about High Falls Gorge, the local summer hangout and had been with her that day in July when she'd

19

first met Jake. Amber couldn't believe such places existed and was deeply impressed with its beauty. She'd even brought her parents and sisters the next day. Her mother, Patsy, a freelance photographer, had spent most of the day snapping pictures while the rest of the family explored all the gorge had to offer.

"Sandy, if you think Ryan is so great, why don't you go after him?" Amber asked out of curiosity.

Sandy stopped to rest. "Well," she replied softly, "I've got my eyes on someone else at the moment."

"Oh, really," Amber said, interested now since this was the first she'd heard about a potential boyfriend. "And who might this lucky boy be, pray tell?"

Sandy looked around, looking for potential spies. "I'm keeping everything on the down-low just in case it doesn't work out, but he's much more mature than Ryan."

Amber laughed. "Okay, so that must make him…what? A third grader?"

They walked another five minutes in companionable silence before Amber veered off the path and hopped onto a big rock. She reached down to pull Sandy up beside her. "Look how pretty everything is," she said in a whisper. The leaves had begun to change, and the girls took a moment to take in the beauty of the bright reds, yellows, and oranges. Amber thought of her mother then and made a mental note to tell her to return to the gorge to take more pictures.

They were near the top now, and laughter rolled down to them, so they jumped off the rock. Amber quickened her pace only to trip unceremoniously on a tree root that had been partially covered with leaves. One hot pink flip-flop sailed into the air as she regained her balance, and she wondered, once again, why she hadn't worn sneakers.

Sandy clutched her sides and shook with silent laughter. Amber stood watching, her hands on her hips. "Are you quite through?" she asked, feigning anger at her friend's callousness.

A loud snort erupted from Sandy, and she quickly covered her mouth with her hand. "That was the least graceful thing I've ever seen," she finally managed to gasp between more bouts of laugher. She wiped the tears from her eyes, bent over, and tossed the wayward flip-flop to Amber.

Amber caught it easily and said a quick prayer of thanks that Ryan had been nowhere in sight. He would have never let her live down that spectacle. "Do you *really* want to talk about graceful? You just snorted like a pig about to be butchered."

"Oh, c'mon...my grandma says my laugh is charming," Sandy said with a huge grin.

Amber slipped her sandal back on and, within a few minutes, they reached a small clearing that served as a picnic area. The path to the falls swept to the left, so Amber almost didn't see him seated at one of the weathered picnic tables situated beneath the protective arms of a big oak tree. His back was turned to her, so he had no idea she stood there, studying him. Amber tapped Sandy and put her fingers to her lips and pointed at Jake. Sandy gave her a thumbs-up and continued along the trail alone; she knew Amber wanted to be alone with Jake.

Amber used the time to catch her breath from the steep climb. She could tell that something was bothering Jake. He was never without Ryan or Adam and was always joking around and teasing them. He now sat hunched over, fiddling absently with a pinecone. An invisible cord pulled Amber toward him. He finally looked up when he heard the murmur of her footsteps in the leaves. She sat down across from him. "What's wrong, Jake? Did someone steal your birthday?" Amber asked lightly.

He smiled at her, but it was a pathetic facsimile of the real thing. "Hey, Amber, I was hoping you'd show up."

"Where are the other two stooges?" Amber asked curiously as she looked around. "I've never seen you without at least one of them."

Jake shrugged his shoulders and pointed absently in the direction of the trail. "They're over there somewhere. I think Ryan's planning on doing a jump. I told them I was waiting for you."

"I bet that made Ryan happy," Amber replied sarcastically. When her response didn't even register a smile, she turned serious. "Are you sure nothing's bothering you? Nothing at all?"

Jake looked at Amber and said, "Nothing's wrong...really." Jake's mind spun with possible explanations. "I guess I'm just mad at Mrs. Drake. She just dropped this huge assignment on us, and I'm trying to figure out how to find the time to do it. I've got cross-

22

country practice, and I have a lot of chores to do around the farm. It's not going to be easy." Jake had already used this excuse with Adam earlier, so it rolled quite naturally off his tongue.

Amber threw her hands in the air. She felt immensely relieved. "Is that all? I thought someone must have been dying from the look on your face. Now get up; let's jump off the bridge, you pansy. This will be our last chance before all the snow starts flying." Amber turned her back on Jake and started jogging up the trail to the bridge where all the others had gathered.

Jake watched her leave and smiled. How could he possibly mope around when she was nearby? *Stop looking so depressed or people will ask questions*, he demanded of himself. *You'll figure out what to do later.* Jake tried to reassure himself as he got up and headed back to the trail. It was a sunny 70-degree afternoon, an unusual occurrence for this time of year. Jake knew the water would be cold, but he didn't care. He wasn't about to be called a pansy by the girl of his dreams.

When he reached the group on the bridge, he found Ryan standing atop the wide wooden railing. He was wearing colorful, Hawaiian print swim trunks and making a huge production of his upcoming jump, attempting to impress a cluster of freshmen girls. They giggled and blushed, and Ryan soaked up the attention like a sponge. He turned his back to the crowd and flexed his muscles. Just as he was about to leap, Jake heard Amber yell, "Too bad your mouth is still your biggest muscle!" Everyone around her laughed as

Ryan, now off-balance and arms windmilling, more or less fell gracelessly off the railing and into the water 80 feet below.

Amber leaned over the railing just in time to see Ryan's splash. She pretended to hold a microphone in her hand, faced the crowd and, imitating an ESPN broadcaster, announced loudly, "Ouch…that might have just cost him the gold." Amber glanced back over her shoulder and down to the water. "But wait...what's this? Folks, I don't believe it. Ryan Chapin has totally redeemed himself with this new stunning bit of athleticism. He's definitely a contender in these Olympic games," she stated seriously. "That marvelous post-dive spectacle was called "Giving the Bird" and is not to be confused with the "Full Moon" which this fine specimen is portraying at this moment."

A few girls hooted and whistled while Ryan did his famous summersaults sans bathing suit. "Who's next?" Ryan yelled up to the crowd as he swam his way to shore. "Hey, dyke, why don't you go?" Ryan looked up eighty feet to his friends on the bridge and taunted, "Let's see how big your balls are!"

"Well, I've already learned from your last three girlfriends that they're bigger than yours," Amber said, once again making the bystanders laugh. She quickly stripped out of her shorts and tank top and passed them to Sandy. Adam stood nearby, staring open-mouthed at Amber who now wore only a bright yellow bikini. As she passed by him she scolded, "What have I told you about staring, Adam?"

"You said it makes me look like a creeper and that I should stop." Adam smiled his lopsided grin. "You should probably know that I have no intention of stopping, though. Shall I hold the lady's sunglasses?" he asked with a bow.

Amber shook her head. "You're impossible," she muttered as she handed over her favorite pair of hot pink shades. She climbed onto the railing and turned to Jake. "I'll see you down there, right?" Without even waiting for a response, she turned toward the water and jumped in, arms crossed over her chest and toes pointed elegantly.

"I know you've got the hots for her," Adam told Jake, "but, wow--I love her even more if that's possible," he said, now wearing Amber's sunglasses and looking over the railing to see Amber surface and begin swimming to shore. He waved to her when she climbed onto a boulder, and she waved back. He turned back to Jake and quipped, "I have to admit…a little piece of me wished that she'd lost her bathing suit top."

"Why are you such a pervert? I mean, you're even starting to creep *me* out," Jake said, amused at his friend.

"Yeah, yeah…I'll be the dirty old man at the mall preying on unsuspecting teenage girls with big boobies. I know that, I've accepted that, and I'll learn to live with that. Now stop stalling. It's your turn, buddy," Adam said to Jake. "You don't want to look like a chicken, do you?"

Actually, Jake was a bit afraid. He'd only jumped from the bridge twice before, and it was terrifying both times. The drop seemed endless. It was scary waiting to hit the water, and it did hurt too. He didn't care how nonchalant Ryan always was when he exited the water. The huge red marks all over his body were testament enough to the overwhelming force with which one hit the water. He took a deep breath to steady his nerves. "Here, hold *my* sunglasses, big boy," he said giving them to Adam, glad for his sudden bravado. "Maybe I'll lose my suit on purpose just for you." Jake winked. He felt one hundred percent better than he had only minutes before.

"That's quite all right. I don't think you'll look as good as Amber," Adam retorted.

Jake blew his friend a kiss and climbed onto the railing. "I bequeath my baseball cards and collection of Playboys to Adam if I don't make it," he called out to an amused crowd before he jumped.

"Wait—you have a collection of Playboys?" Adam asked, racing toward the railing. He looked back at the crowd and said, "I can't believe he's been holding out on me all these years. What kind of friend does that to a guy?" Adam didn't wait for an answer and was already running down the trail back to the lake to question Jake.

*   *   *

Jake and Amber sat away from Ryan, Adam, and a few other kids from school. Most of the others had gone home. It was about seven o'clock, and the fire Ryan had started provided most of the light now that the sun had begun to set. Jake watched the shadows dance across Amber's pretty face. He had forgotten about the assignment that had tormented him earlier that day. Well, he hadn't entirely forgotten about it; he'd simply pushed the thought of it to the back of

26

his brain for the time being. Jake was about to ask Amber to be his girlfriend when he heard footsteps approaching.

Adam appeared out of the darkness, his hands in his pockets. Timidly, he began, "Jake, I only want to borrow..."

Jake responded slowly as if he were speaking to a complete idiot, "Adam, read my lips. I do not now, nor have I ever had a collection of Playboys. You'd be the first to know if I did. I was just fooling around. Now please, leave us alone for five minutes," Jake said patiently.

"Okay. I just wanted to make sure," he responded glumly. Adam slunk back to the group where he was teased mercilessly about his glossy centerfold wife-to-be. Adam was too good-natured to feel badly. He was teased a lot because he was so goofy; he was famous for saying the wrong thing at the wrong time. He was fairly good looking with sandy blond hair and green eyes. He was five seven with an athletic build, but he was simply too awkward to have a serious girlfriend. All the girls just wanted to be friends with him because, even though he was sometimes embarrassing to be around, he was extremely kind and funny. He was always very attractive...until he spoke and said something absolutely stupid.

"Hey, Adam, did you bring marshmallows, or what?" Jodi asked impatiently.

"They're in the car," Adam said, making no move to get them and continuing to poke the fire with a thick stick.

Ryan shook his head in disbelief. "Don't you think we should go get them?" Ryan asked, his voice dripping with sarcasm. He rolled his eyes at the others and grabbed Adam by the hood of his sweatshirt. As the two boys walked away from the others, Ryan asked, "What's Jake doing with Amber over there all alone?"

"They were just talking quietly. I didn't exactly eavesdrop," Adam replied sheepishly.

"Yeah, I know. You were too busy thinking about all that lost time with the playmates, huh, Hef?" he asked grinning. "All kidding aside…do you think they're going to get together? I don't think I approve. She's such a bitch. How are we supposed to hang out if she's tagging along all the time?"

"Ryan, she's only a bitch to you because you're an asshole to her. If you gave her a chance you'd see that she's pretty cool. You only hate her because she hasn't fallen all over herself trying to impress you. You're just not used to that. Plus, her dad could give you some pointers that could really improve your game."

"My game is already perfect," Ryan said arrogantly.

"Yeah, right," Adam responded sarcastically. "I can think of quite a few turnovers from last season that you could probably do without this year." He pulled open the car door, reached inside, and pulled out a brown grocery bag. "Here." He shoved the bag into Ryan's chest. "Now let's go," he said, gently shoving Ryan back the way they'd come. "I wanna get back…I think Jodi likes me. She lets me do her French homework for her, so she must be interested, right?"

"In your dreams, Romeo." The two carefully made their way down the winding trail. The temperature had dropped significantly, but everyone now wore warm clothes, and the fire made the evening quite cozy. Ryan's flashlight skipped over the narrow path, barely illuminating its rocky surface. "It sure is dark out here." He spun around and flashed the light into Adam's eyes. "Are you scared, Adam?" Ryan asked trying his best to sound like a deranged axe murderer.

Adam stopped abruptly and held up his hands in an attempt to shield his eyes from the sudden blinding light. "You're such a dick. I don't even know why I let you hang out with me."

Ryan scoffed haughtily. "Let's get something straight, you douche. I let *you* hang out with *me*." He turned back around and continued down the path. "I'm actually quite surprised you haven't fallen on your face by now, Adam. You're not exactly known for your coordination."

"Well, I was definitely a lot better off before you blinded me with your flashlight. I can't see jack shit right now," Adam grumbled as he stepped on Ryan's heels.

"Jesus, Adam, do you have to follow so closely?"

"I'm so sorry to invade your precious personal space, Ryan. Maybe you should have brought another flashlight." Sometimes he found great pleasure in annoying his friend. He was glad the darkness masked his grin.

"Yeah, well, if I happen to feel your hand on my ass, so help me, I'll beat you so badly your father won't recognize you," murmured Ryan.

Adam laughed. "Don't worry. I got more than enough of your ass when you mooned everyone earlier today. Not everyone finds you as attractive as you find yourself."

*   *   *

Amber was glad that Jake was in a better mood. Something had really been bothering him earlier, and she doubted if his foul mood was the result of a biology assignment. She didn't worry too much since he was acting more like himself now. They sat atop a picnic table huddled together and wrapped in the fleece blanket she'd grabbed from her trunk. In order to get some time alone, they'd had to leave the warmth of the fire.

Amber snuggled closer to Jake. She really liked everything about him—he was smart, polite, thoughtful, and kind—all the traits that were almost impossible to find in a boy these days. Most of the boys she met were all swagger and cockiness, like Ryan. She really thought Jake felt the same way about her, but she'd waited all summer for him to ask her out, and he still hadn't done it. They'd spent a lot of time getting to know each other—mostly at group outings and in the classes they shared at school, and she was getting frustrated. "You know, Jake, I really like hanging out with you, but I still can't understand why you socialize with that Neanderthal, Ryan. Despite that one repulsive decision, you're a pretty nice guy."

"Thanks, I guess," Jake uttered. He felt his face warm at the compliment.

An uncomfortable silence ensued. "Oh, hell!" Amber blurted out. "Are you ever going to get the guts to ask me out?" Now it was Amber's turn to blush. The night's shadows hid her discomfort, but she looked away from Jake anyway, immediately regretting her rash decision. *What if he doesn't feel the same way?* she worried.

Jake turned Amber's face toward his before wrapping her cold hands in his. "I've actually been trying to get up the nerve all night to ask you," he said smiling.

Relief flooded Amber. "Really?" she asked, turning to look into Jake's gray-blue eyes. "I know I wasn't all that romantic, but…"

"You are perfect," Jake whispered, and he pulled her close to kiss her.

CHAPTER 2

Jake had just finished his Saturday morning chores in the barn. He kicked his boots against the concrete step leading to the mudroom. Chunks of mud and manure that had clung stubbornly inside his boot treads now littered the grass. His grandmother had trained him very well not to track cow manure into the house. He'd been a fast learner after he'd been forced to mop up his mess from the kitchen floor…on his hands and knees…with an old rag and bucket of cleaner. His Nana, even though tiny at four feet, seven inches, was a force to be reckoned with, and no one dared to defy her or soil her spotless linoleum.

It was barely eight o'clock, and Jake had already been awake for two hours; he was exhausted. Even though the family farm had grown smaller as his grandfather grew older, it still required a lot of work. The herd consisted mainly of beef cattle, which were sold to the local butcher. They also had some chickens, a couple of pigs (which his grandmother perversely named Bacon and Ham), and various barn cats. There was also a fruit orchard and huge vegetable garden. On weekends, Jake was responsible for feeding the animals, cleaning out stalls, and doing whatever else Nana asked him to do. Now that it was October, all the field work was completed.

He passed through the empty kitchen and climbed the worn, wooden stairs to his room slowly and automatically. He closed the door softly and flopped onto his bed, the springs protesting loudly with a series of squeaks. That morning his alarm clock had blasted him awake and out of his dream-world, back to an appalling biology assignment that was going to force him to face his past. The good feelings he'd experienced with Amber just hours ago had been replaced with dread. He definitely didn't want to face his past, and he surely didn't want anyone finding out about what had happened ten years earlier.

Jake contemplated not doing the assignment at all, but good grades were important to him. He *had* to go to college; he had no intention of working on the family farm. He had big plans for himself. He wanted to become a pharmacist. Biology and chemistry were his favorite subjects, and he wanted to help people with his chosen profession. Making tons of money was a pretty good incentive as well. He knew that excellent science grades were necessary to be accepted into such an arduous program, so there was no way he could blow off this major assignment. His goal was to repay his grandparents for their many years of kindness by supporting them financially so they could relax and enjoy a leisurely retirement without feeling the strain of working the farm. Farming was a tough lifestyle, and Jake wanted his grandparents to travel and enjoy each other's company while they still could. They were already in their early sixties and money was always tight. It's not as if farmers got a pension plan. At the moment, they lived an almost subsistent lifestyle, but Jake didn't know how long they would be able to maintain their workload as they neared their seventies, especially once he left for college.

Jake let his thoughts stray to his past, a life he longed to forget but was forced to relive over and over in his nightmares. When the sting of tears pricked his eyes, he sat up abruptly and determinedly made his way to his closet. He quickly pulled open the door and forcibly parted his clothing, allowing him to see the back wall. He moved with purpose before he could chicken out. A door, about the size of a shoebox, was now visible in the back corner near the floor. Jake eased the heavy closet door shut behind him. The light from the bare bulb glared obscenely. Getting down on his hands and knees, he crawled toward the tiny door, the knees of his jeans whispering against the old plank floor. It opened easily, swinging inward at his gentle push. All of his movements were tender now, almost reverent, as though he'd entered a sacred place. He had no idea what the original purpose of this tiny opening had once been, but he'd used it to horde his secrets ever since he'd called his grandparent's farm his home.

He leaned toward the opening, his arm disappearing completely inside. When he pulled back his arm, he was clutching a small wooden box. Jake stared at the unopened box for what seemed an eternity. He pulled down his sleeve so that it covered his hand and gently wiped away a layer of dust. Carved into the top of the mahogany box were the initials *E.J.D.* Jake traced the intricate lettering over and over, leaned back against the wall, and stared up at the ceiling. Tears burned his eyes as the box laid, a silent torment, in his lap. Finally, Jake looked down, wiped away the tears that rolled down his cheeks, and opened the box.

"Jake, why aren't you eating? Do you feel sick?" asked Nana at the breakfast table. She felt his forehead for a fever. Jake found tranquility in her calloused hands and allowed her to baby him. "You don't feel warm, so what hurts?"

That was typical Nana. She was a no-nonsense woman who always wanted to get right down to business. "I don't think I slept well. That's all," Jake replied, but he could still feel the weight of the box in his hands.

"Well, what time did you come home? I was out like a light right after *Wheel of Fortune.*"

"I didn't stay out too late. I was in bed by 10:30," Jake responded. He pushed his pancakes around his plate before dutifully taking another bite.

Nana bustled about the small kitchen, making another pile of pancakes for her husband who was checking on a new calf. She chattered amiably. "That Pat Sajak is just so cute, but I still think Vanna's after his money. I wonder how much she gets paid to flaunt her goodies like that. I'd do it for free just to be near Pat." Nana laughed heartily.

"If he didn't fire Vanna for you, he'd be an idiot." He couldn't quite understand his grandmother's fascination with the game show host, but it was hilarious to watch her ogle the TV screen and make snide comments about his attractive co-host. Sometimes she reminded him of Adam. That's probably why they always got along so well.

35

"Did you have fun with your little friends, dear? Was that handsome Ryan with you?" she asked coyly.

"Yes, Nana, and he sends his regards," Jake replied with a smile. His Nana made him laugh, and a laugh was just what he needed. She always complained about getting old and what a horror the ordeal was. She insisted that age had faded her once bright blue eyes to gray, and her now wrinkled, leathery skin had once been as smooth and white as ivory. Papa always just looked away and smiled when she went on one of her rants.

Jake had seen old photographs of his grandparents when they were first married. Even Jake had to admit that the old black and whites didn't do justice to his grandmother's beauty. Nana would point at the picture and brag about her long, lush raven-black hair and tell stories about how the boys would pine for her. Papa would just roll his eyes in response. Her long, mostly-gray hair was now almost always pulled up into a bun, which made her appear austere when she was anything but. She was a short woman. Tiny, in fact and getting shorter every day, she'd joke, but she made up for her short stature with her fiery personality. Jake thought, *Well, I definitely don't get my height from Nana, but maybe some of my sense of humor comes from her.* Jake couldn't help but wonder if personality traits were truly inherited or simply learned from one's environment.

Jake jerked upright in his chair when he suddenly realized that he was unconsciously thinking about his biology assignment. *Maybe this won't be so bad after all,* Jake thought. He gulped down his orange juice in three swallows, polished off his blueberry pancakes, and made his way to his room. As Jake climbed the stairs, he was troubled by a nagging premonition that this biology project would be the end of the peaceful life he'd come to love.

*   *   *

Amber sleepily stretched in her rumpled bed. A smile stretched across her face when she thought about the previous night. Kissing Jake had been wonderful. He hadn't been like the other boys she'd kissed. Their kisses had been so sloppy and forceful, complete failures in her mind. Jake's kisses, on the other hand, were tender and sweet and left her wanting more. He also didn't try to grope her like some kind of wild orangutan jam-packed with testosterone.

She remembered how Ryan and Adam had broken the spell, stumbling clumsily down the dark trail with marshmallows. She smiled at the memory. Even those two knuckleheads hadn't ruined her night. In fact, Amber reveled in the fact that she'd ruined Ryan's night. Once he'd seen them kissing and had completed his totally lame performance of retching in the bushes, he'd been relatively silent for the rest of the evening, sulking. Of course, he had still hung out with Sandy, mostly staring at her huge boobs and occasionally making a smartass remark, so maybe his night hadn't been wrecked after all. She was glad that Sandy wasn't in to Ryan, but it would be funny to see him rejected by a lowly freshman. *Man, I must really hate him,* she thought to herself.

Spencer, Amber's cocker spaniel, came tunneling out from beneath the covers. He began licking her face furiously, a sure sign of needing the closest tree, so she yanked the covers off herself and sailed down the stairs. Amber's parents, Ben and Patsy Green, were decorating the front porch with pumpkins, an assortment of gourds, and dried cornstalks when Spencer streaked past them, a yellow blur, and ran around the house to the backyard to do his business.

Amber had been ecstatic when her parents told her they were moving away from Syracuse. Even though it was the only home she'd known, she never really felt like she'd belonged. There were so many kids in her school that only two teachers knew her by name, and she'd had to walk through a metal detector each morning. Her father had always liked northern New York and had often gone on fishing trips with his grandfather to Lake Ozonia, so when he retired, he'd decided that the country would be the best place to raise his three daughters.

Now they had eighty acres all to themselves, wild deer coming to drink from the small brook that meandered through the woods out back, no traffic noises, and the cutest little dog ever. Amber watched from the kitchen window as Spencer sprinted from one tree to another. As she poured herself a glass of orange juice, she could hear her mother laugh and then her father shout, "Spencer, cut it out!" Amber grabbed a banana and headed out the front door to see her father attempting to wrestle a corn stalk out of Spencer's mouth.

Amber called out, "Good morning, Mom and Dad." She nodded approvingly as she took in the fall decorations. "I see you've caught the Halloween spirit. It looks good out here…very festive," she said beaming. She just couldn't stop smiling, and it was all

38

because of Jake. She sat down on the porch swing and watched as her father finally won the tug-of-war battle against the dog.

"Did you have a good time last night, Amber?" her mom asked. She wore old jeans and a ratty old Syracuse University sweatshirt that bore the stains of many painting misadventures.

"Yes, I certainly did, and it's now official," Amber said smiling widely.

"You mean Jake finally got the courage to ask you out?" Patsy Green gushed, coming to sit beside her daughter. Unlike many of her friends, Patsy actually had a great relationship with her teenaged daughter, but she always wondered how long Amber would keep up an open line of communication with her.

"Well, not quite. I had to take the initiative," Amber said sheepishly. "It turns out Jake was a lot shyer than we estimated, but I just couldn't wait around forever. You know…I'm not getting any younger," she joked.

"Time out here," Ben stated sharply. "Who's Jake, and why haven't I heard about him before?" He pulled a rocking chair close to his daughter and sat down heavily, having finally succeeded in tying the unwieldy stalks to the porch's columns. Spencer jumped onto his lap and turned around three times before finally settling down with a huff.

Both Amber and her mother looked exasperatingly at each other. "Ben, for crying out loud, she's been talking non-stop about Jake since we moved here. It would be nice if you'd mute ESPN occasionally and listen to what your daughters have to say."

Ben smirked. "Maybe I just have selective hearing and don't want to admit that my little baby is growing up."

"Oh, please, Dad." Amber rolled her eyes. Her father always treated her like a child. Sometimes it was cute, like when she needed something, but it was pretty embarrassing when he talked like that in front of her friends. "You still have two other daughters you can baby."

"I know, but you'll always be my first little darling." He reached out to pat her head, but she ducked. "Now…tell me about this Jake character. Am I going to have to answer the door with my shotgun or in my underwear?" Ben put his finger to his lips and pretended to think deeply.

"If you do either of those things, I'll simply have to tell Jake that you are my crazy uncle who recently escaped from a mental institution," replied Amber as she smiled at her father. She turned to her mother. "Mom, it's your duty to keep your husband under control. I don't want dad's tighty whities scaring away Jake…or the entire neighborhood, for that matter."

*   *   *

Adam Krovlovski tossed and turned in his king-sized bed. He lived only about a mile from Amber in a huge white house that sat back from the road. The kids at school always teased Adam about being rich, but he never let his father's money go to his head. He received an allowance of one hundred dollars each week, but he rarely spent it all, preferring, instead, to treat his friends to lunch or deposit it into his bank account. He could understand why everyone would tease him; it's not like his father was discreet about his wealth.

Once a high-profile attorney in New York City, Blake Allen Krovlovski, Esq. had transplanted his family five years ago to the tiny town of Bangor. He'd purchased close to two hundred acres of land for next to nothing from a farmer going out of business. A team of builders had demolished the previous farmhouse and constructed an absolutely amazing three-story brick mansion, but it certainly didn't fit in with the other houses in this rural, impoverished community. A precisely pruned, tall cedar hedge afforded Blake the privacy he sought and prevented him from having to look at his neighbors' hideous houses. Stately white pillars stood sentry beside two enormous, mahogany doors. In the center of the circular driveway, beautiful koi swam lazily in a giant stone fountain. Two full-time gardeners kept the lawn perfectly manicured and lush with vegetation. Not a single blade of crabgrass or stray dandelion dared to sully Blake's yard. Inside, everything was state-of-the-art. Most of the rooms, such as the billiards and trophy rooms, were totally unnecessary and never occupied. Adam knew that his father only viewed the house as one more status symbol--another way to exhibit his fortune. They even had their own tennis and basketball courts, a heated in-ground pool and an outdoor Jacuzzi tub, which were flawlessly maintained by Pasquel, the handyman Mrs. Krovlovski #2 had hired last year. Rumor had it that Pasquel and Julia spent a lot of time in that swimming pool, and they weren't exactly cleaning it.

41

Blake still practiced law, but he didn't work nearly as hard as he had in the city. In his opinion, he was better able to manipulate these ordinary, unsuspecting people. "They're too stupid to even know when they've been duped," he told Adam all too often.

Adam couldn't stand the way Blake treated his clients. He'd seen his father take advantage of way too many people simply to earn more money. Blake was already one of the richest individuals in all of Franklin County, but greed was his one true love.

Sleep was an obstacle that Adam could not overcome. He usually only got between four to five hours of sleep each night. Looking at his alarm clock, he realized he'd been lying in bed for the last three hours, willing his mind to stop churning. Unfortunately, it was impossible to escape one's own relentless thoughts. They just kept coming, unremitting in their attack. His curtains were open slightly, and he watched the sky turn from light gray to rosy pink. Mostly his mind turned to his dysfunctional family and his plan to escape it all when he went to college.

The only family member who had loved Adam unconditionally was Gigi, his grandmother on his mother's side. She had been his saving grace after his parents' divorce. She was the reason why Adam was nothing like his father, mother, or older brothers. She was a big woman, always warm and soft and full of love, all the things lacking in Adam's childhood.

His parents had officially divorced when he was eight, but his mother had been absent for most of his life. He remembered that she had blond hair, liked to sing in the car, and smelled like cough medicine. Adam later found out that his mother was an alcoholic and had spent a lot of his youth in and out of rehab facilities. The last time he saw her was from his bedroom window. She had been screaming at his father down below on the sidewalk. A yellow taxi waited nearby, its back door still open, the driver tactfully ignoring the chaotic scene playing out before him. Adam hadn't been able to make out his mother's words, but her face was bright red and she gesticulated wildly. He watched as his father laughed and tossed some money into her face. She scrambled on her hands and knees to collect the cash, yelled at Blake's retreating back, entered the yawning mouth of the taxi, and slammed the door. She hadn't even waved goodbye. That was nine years ago.

Between the ages of four and eight, Adam had spent the majority of his life with his grandmother who lived on the next block. He had been the lucky one—his older brothers had lived with their father, but Blake had had no patience for his youngest son. Thankfully, Gigi had been more than happy to take him in. He stayed with her during the week and spent many weekends with her, along with his brothers, when Blake was off with one of his many "girlfriends."

That's when he learned about kindness, respect, and integrity. She told him stories where good overcame evil and where gallant princes saved ladies in distress. As Adam grew older, his father wanted him back. "What are you doing to my son? You're making him soft," Blake used to growl at Gigi. Adam now realized that she was taking every opportunity to make him human. She oftentimes brought him to volunteer at a nearby thrift store and soup kitchen. They had their best talks then, sometimes while sorting through a mountain of clothes in a musty, dank storeroom or while elbow-deep in soapsuds in a steamy kitchen. Even at six, he quickly learned about those who have everything, like himself, and those who lack even the basics. "Your father would never help these people," Gigi would tell him as she nodded toward the shoppers at the front of the store. "He thinks their hard luck is their fault. But, and you have to always remember this, each one of these people has a story. Until you know that story, Adam, you can't pass judgment on their circumstances. You're lucky that you have clothes, shelter, food, and love, but not everyone is as fortunate as you."

When Gigi died four years ago, one year after he'd been uprooted from the city and deposited in the middle of nowhere, he'd thought his heart would break. He hadn't even known she'd been sick. A letter, a box of photos, and a few children's books had arrived from her lawyer two months after she'd died. "Why didn't we go to her funeral," Adam had screamed at his father.

"I was out of town," he'd retorted cold-heartedly.

Adam had vowed then that he would never be like his father. He believed that Blake was filled with a cold evil that had already infected his two older brothers, but he promised himself and his grandmother that he would avoid its venomous bite. He did everything in his power to avoid his brothers, his father, and his STD-riddled stepmother. Thankfully, it wasn't hard to do in such a big house.

Even though he despised him, Adam still felt a twisted need to earn his father's approval. The worst part about his father was seeing the looks of disgust and disappointment flash across his open face. He never even attempted to mask his emotions—he was an open book with even a reference page for easy reading. It had happened only once in the five years since they'd moved to Bangor. It was a sudden burst of violence against his brother that had earned him a pat on the back and a congratulatory smile. "That's right, Adam, to be a man you have to fight back," he'd said proudly as his other son wiped blood from his lip.

As different as Adam was from his father, he had to admit that his brothers were spitting images of the man, both in looks and personality. Charles and Justin had their father's muscular build, squared jaw, dark complexion, and height. They both were a few inches taller than Adam.

Charles was twenty and a junior at the University of Syracuse. He was studying to be a lawyer like his old man. Justin was still living at home, a senior in high school. Neither of his two brothers ever had any problem attracting girls. Their good looks, combined with natural confidence and fat wallets, lured the female population like blood attracted sharks. They actually had a competition going to see who could "bag the most chicks" by the age of twenty-one. Adam was disgusted when the two would get together to brag about their most recent conquests. Sex was just a sport to them, the girls merely pawns in their sick game. Adam tried to stay away from both of them at all costs. Blake, however, was proud of his two strapping, virile sons.

Adam wanted to be nothing like his brothers. He knew his pick-up lines were stupid, and he knew his immature behavior was less than attractive, but he was perfectly content with being "just friends" with his female classmates (for now anyway). All of the lewd comments he made to Jake and Ryan were nothing but male bluster, an expectation of his friends. He'd been acting like that for so long now that it was part of his personality. Over the years, it had become harder to remove the mask he wore. That was one more reason he was excited for college; he would be able to reinvent himself—shed his disguise and be more of who he really wanted to be.

As his room began to brighten with the rising sun, Adam attempted to relive the fun of last night and realized how lucky he was to have such good friends. Even though Ryan gave him a hard time, he still made him feel like he was a part of something. As far as Adam was concerned, Jake and Ryan were more like a family than his own. He knew that the kids in his class thought of him as an awkward goofball, but at least they thought of him, which was more than he could say for his own father or brothers. He tried to steer his thoughts to Jodi, but he was interrupted by a loud banging on his door.

"Hey, fag, you up yet?" Justin's raspy voice was unmistakable through the door. "You need to bring me to Split Rock so I can pick up my car." Split Rock just happened to be the most popular party place for teens, and after Justin's last run-in with the law two months ago, when he'd put his car in the ditch, he had promised his father never to drink and drive again. He figured that forcing his loser brother to pick up his car was a small price to pay.

Justin had been duly impressed with the way his father played those small town cops and had proudly given Adam a play by play report when he'd returned home. Daddy Dearest had come flying to his rescue, miraculously saving him from a police record. Justin had only spent fifteen minutes in a holding cell before his father arrived. He hadn't even lost driving privileges. All it took was a little money greasing the right person's palm and Justin was home free.

Adam knew that his brothers would always rely on their father and his money to get them out of trouble. Justin hadn't been taught a lesson; he'd only learned that his father would bail him out time and time again. Adam opened his bedroom door a crack. "I haven't showered yet. Why don't you ask one of your girlfriends to take you?" he replied. It was nine o'clock, and Adam could still smell the stench of alcohol on his brother's breath.

Justin roughly shoved open the door. "I have to pick up Sandy at ten. She's coming over for some swimming lessons," he said with a wink.

Adam sat at his desk, then looked back at his brother, confused. "Wait…Sandy-- the freshman? The one who lives three houses down? Can't she just walk over here?"

"That wouldn't be very gentlemanly now, would it," Justin smirked as he bent over to pick up a rumpled pair of jeans off the

47

floor. He crumpled them into a ball and whipped them at Adam who caught them right before they slammed into his face. "So what *I* need is for *you* to get your lazy ass moving and take me to get my car."

"You could at least ask politely, you know. You don't have to be such a dick all the time," Adam mumbled as he pulled on the jeans.

"What did you say?" Justin asked fiercely, stepping toward Adam with his hands clenched tightly.

Adam knew better than to repeat what he'd said. "Nothing. Let's just go," he mumbled as he grabbed a t-shirt from his dresser and headed for the door. Justin disgusted him; Sandy was just a freshman. Ryan had been flirting with her just last night at the gorge. What was she doing with his brother? Ryan would be pissed when he found out that Justin had Sandy on his radar.

CHAPTER 3

The electric razor buzzed across his skin, the droning sound amplified by the tiny room. Ever since he'd come to this place, his hearing had become more acute. He was more aware of his surroundings and of people's movements. Then again, he had to be in order to survive.

The man turned on the faucet and watched as the water circled around the rusted drain before disappearing forever with an unsettling gurgling noise. He stared at his pasty-white palms before submerging them. The stream of cool water sluiced through his fingers as he stared at his reflection in the mirror. He was mesmerized by the majesty of his own eyes. The blue irises were flecked with hazel specks, which seemed to float slowly around the pupil.

A loud thump and an angry shout brought him unwillingly back from his trance. His mask slowly slid back into place. He cupped his hands together, catching handfuls of water, and splashed them on his now tingling face. He grabbed his grimy towel from the edge of the sink. He studied his face in the mirror as rivulets of water trickled down his cheeks to his chin where they hung for a second, suspended, before falling freely to the concrete floor.

He dried his face and then stood with his legs firmly planted apart. His hands grasped the metal rim of the sink. His dark brown hair was shorn close to his head; the thin material of his tee-shirt strained against his biceps and broad chest. He was almost handsome, but there was something about his eyes that frightened people. They were empty...devoid of feeling or expression. It was impossible to read his mood by looking at his eyes. He stared at the mirror and traced the thick, puckered scar that marred his throat, and he remembered.

He settled onto the edge of his bed and leaned forward, his elbows resting on his knees. He rocked back and forth slowly, swaying his head to an invisible melody. His eyes were closed and he looked almost content, soothed by a lullaby of memory. A serene smile curled his lips as he opened his eyes back to his reality. He liked to remember the way things used to be; he hated to think of how everything turned out. He focused on the drops of water that now marred the floor near the sink. The rounded edges were so distinct against the concrete, a near-black against a light-gray. He settled onto his bed and was swallowed by memory.

CHAPTER 4

It was Thursday, and Jake and Ryan were cleaning up after their biology lab. Jake couldn't believe that almost an entire week had passed since he and Amber had begun dating. Even though they were both busy with sports—Jake with cross-country and Amber with volleyball—they still managed to spend some time together each night. They never ran out of things to say to each other and shared a similar sense of humor which kept them laughing most of the time. Jake absently put the supplies back in the cupboard at the back of the room and gathered up his lab papers.

Ryan snapped his fingers an inch away from Jake's face, disturbing him from his daydream. "Wake up," he snapped. "Are you going to let me copy your lab tonight, or should I get it before homeroom tomorrow?"

"What are you talking about, Ryan?" Jake asked, perturbed.

"Um…duh! I need to copy the lab results." Ryan was being obnoxious and pretending to use sign language which consisted of a whole lot of middle fingers.

Jake couldn't hide his irritation, but it was his own fault for letting Ryan be his lab partner. "Hey, ass-wipe," he said softly so Mrs. Drake wouldn't overhear, "why didn't you write down the information as we did the lab? Is that a concept your little brain can't comprehend?"

Ryan put out his hands like a crossing guard stopping traffic. "Whoa. Slow down, buddy." He shook his head slowly back and forth before coming to stand beside Jake. Ryan slipped his arm around his friend's shoulders and continued as though auditioning for a daytime soap opera. "What's with all of this fighting? I don't think I can take much more of it, Jake." He wiped at non-existent tears and sniffled.

Jake smiled as his curious classmates began to stare. He reassured them,

"Nothing to see here...just another moment brought to you by Ryan Chapin."

Ryan interrupted loudly, loving the attention, "It's that girl. She's trying to come between us." He clasped his hands together to make a desperate plea. "You've got to end it, Jake. Do it for me...for us?"

The kids in the class loved to watch Ryan's inane performances and began a polite golf clap. Mrs. Drake, meanwhile, silently glided behind Ryan and tapped his shoulder.

Ryan startled and placed his hand over his heart. "You must be some sort of ninja, Mrs. Drake. You practically gave me heart attack." He bent low with his hands on his knees and breathed deeply. "Maybe I should go to the nurse."

"Mr. Chapin, your performance has ended. Take a bow and return to your seat so that I may finish class." As she made her way to the front of the classroom, Jake heard her mumble, "Or I might just use some of my ninja moves on you."

Jake hid his smile behind his hand.

Ryan turned to his friend and obnoxiously grumbled, "I think we should tie a bell around her neck so we can hear her coming." He sullenly made his way back to his desk.

Everyone returned to their seats, happy to have a little entertainment. Jake no longer felt annoyed at Ryan. As he finished copying down the notes on the board, he knew that, once again, he'd hand over the lab results to his irresponsible friend.

When the bell rang at the end of class, Mrs. Drake called out, "Mr. Carver, could I speak with you for a moment?"

Jake had been heading out the door with Ryan and was on his way to cross-country practice when he heard Mrs. Drake's shrill voice. "Sure," Jake replied cautiously, wondering what she wanted. He turned back to the teacher's desk, and his stomach dropped as he realized the topic she most likely wanted to discuss.

"Later, buddy. Have fun," Ryan said with a grin at the door, oblivious to his friend's discomfort.

"Why don't you sit down right here," Mrs. Drake stated seriously, pointing to a desk. Her bony frame slipped easily into a student's desk so they could speak face-to-face.

Oh boy, Jake thought, *she's trying to make me comfortable by deigning to sit at a kid's desk. I bet Dr. Phil gave her that advice.* Jake sat in the chair across from Mrs. Drake, trying to appear nonchalant. He could tell that she was nervous because she kept fiddling with the bifocals that hung from the thin chain around her neck. Jake could feel a cool trickle of sweat snake its way down his back. *Please don't say it,* he screamed in his head.

"Jake, I wanted to speak with you about the genetics project I assigned. You've probably been avoiding it, am I right?" she asked.

Jake nodded sheepishly. He was the best student in the class, and it embarrassed him to be thought of as a dreaded slacker.

Mrs. Drake cleared her throat nervously and continued. "I know that this will be difficult for you since you can't interview your parents. However, I do think that you can gather enough evidence from your grandparents. They must have pictures and first hand accounts about your parents." Mrs. Drake continued quickly, almost as eager to finish this terrible moment as Jake. "I realize that this project may bring up some bad memories, but I just wanted you to know that it's a valuable learning tool for this unit. I wouldn't ask you to relive everything if I didn't think it was important," Mrs. Drake finished. She looked up into Jake's eyes for the first time since she'd begun talking. "I don't think it will be as bad as you think, and it might be good for you to deal with some of these issues now that you're older and better equipped to understand them," she added quietly.

Jake looked at his teacher. He knew that she was trying to be helpful, but he said nothing. He didn't trust his voice. It might betray the anguish now crawling up his throat. He nodded instead.

"Don't be worried that the other kids will find out. Your results aren't going to be presented to the class. This project is about discovering how *you* became the person you are today. And trust me;

you're stronger than you think, Jake." Mrs. Drake lightly touched Jake's hand for a second and pushed back her chair. She rose gracefully.

Jake remained anchored in his chair. He looked up at his teacher curiously and finally found his voice. "How do *you* know about it?" He had kept the details of his parents' deaths a secret for so many years that no one ever bothered to ask anymore. He'd only been seven when he'd moved in with his grandparents. His young friends had just accepted his answer for what it was. That was the beauty of childhood—Rebecca has two moms, Devin is adopted, and Jake's parents died. Little kids just aren't big on details, and adults have avoided the topic like the plague, probably suspecting a major emotional breakdown if it were ever mentioned. Surprisingly enough, this was the first time a non-family member or psychologist had ever broached the issue with him.

Mrs. Drake turned away from Jake and swiped a tissue from the box on her desk. Absently, she wiped her glasses as she stalled for time. Jake stared anxiously at her back. When she finally spoke, it was almost a whisper. "I had your mom in school," she said softly. Finally, she turned to face Jake. "She was one of my favorite students."

"Oh," Jake said feeling stupid. He tilted his head to one side and considered his teacher thoughtfully. It had never crossed his mind that Mrs. Drake could have been his mom's teacher, probably because he'd never thought of his mother as a teenager.

She crumpled the tissue in her hand and tossed it into the garbage can next to her desk. Looking down into her now-empty hands, she said, "You actually remind me of Elizabeth quite a bit. You have the same curiosity and work ethic." She smiled and met Jake's gaze. "Your mom actually *enjoyed* learning, just like you. That's becoming a rare attribute these days," she added wryly.

Jake could sense a shift in their student-teacher relationship. He'd always felt there would be some sort of judgment if people knew the truth, a courtroom feeling, accusatory fingers pointing at him, but he felt a level of sympathy and understanding that he'd never expected—almost like a bond. Unfolding his long legs, Jake stood. "Thanks for telling me all of that, Mrs. Drake. I do feel a little better about the project now."

"Good. I'm glad, Jake, and if you ever want to hear some stories about your mom, you know where to find me."

"Someday I'll take you up on that offer," he replied, shy now. "I'll see you tomorrow," he called over his shoulder as he headed for the door. As Jake rushed to the locker room to change for practice, he found an ounce of solace.

*   *   *

"Jake, who were you on the phone with for so long?" Nana asked suspiciously. "Was it that new girlfriend of yours?" she added with a wink as she turned back to the sink of dirty dishes.

Jake had finally realized, with the help of Mrs. Drake, that he couldn't put off the assignment any longer. He had to do the project, so he might just as well finish it as quickly and as painlessly as possible. He thought it would be better to simply rip off the band-aid concealing his past. "I was talking to Grandma and Grandpa Carver." He leaned into the refrigerator and pulled out a Mountain Dew. "I have a biology assignment due next week, and I have to interview my family to find out where I get my unique characteristics." He kept his voice light, but he could see the worry cloud Nana's eyes. He couldn't remember the last time they'd spoken about his mother.

"Oh," she said simply, her smile vanishing. She was taken aback by Jake's blunt explanation and busied herself at the kitchen sink, washing the supper dishes with much more concentration than was necessary. She was thankful for this time to collect her thoughts. She suddenly understood Jake's uneasiness at the breakfast table Saturday morning. She, in turn, felt a lead weight in her stomach. *Is it time for him to know the truth?* she asked herself. *No, we've kept it hidden for so long that he'll hate us if he finds out.*

"I guess I'll need to talk to you and Papa about your parents. Do you want to do it tomorrow night after supper?" Jake asked. "I'm supposed to go back three generations, learn about my relatives, and discover the similarities we share." He prattled on, afraid to stop once he'd forced himself to begin. The last thing he wanted to do was make Nana sad. "I made up a list of questions about physical and personality traits. Maybe you have some pictures you want to show me, and I'd like to hear a story or two about my great-grandparents since they died before I was born."

Jake noticed that his grandmother had been washing the same plate since he'd begun the conversation and became even more worried. Jake's mother had been her only child, and it was obvious that Nana was reliving the nightmare as well. "Nana, are you all right?" Jake asked quietly as he approached her. He placed a hand gently on her shoulder.

"Yes, honey, I'm fine. I was just thinking about where I've kept all those old pictures, that's all." Nana spoke too quickly, and her voice sounded strange to Jake's ears.

Realizing his grandmother was upset, Jake left the kitchen and headed to his room. Over the years, he had learned that it was better to leave Nana alone when she was sad. She would never confide in Jake; she was old-school and determined to solve her problems on her own. As far as Jake could tell, Nana solved her emotional woes by sweeping them under a rug. Guilt crept over Jake, like an ominous shadow, and it made his stomach churn. As he climbed the stairs he thought, *I probably shouldn't have been so direct. I should have eased into the conversation like I did with Grandma and Grandpa Carver. I'm such an idiot.*

He looked at the empty poster board covering his desk and decided that since he couldn't rewind what had just happened, he might as well start with the information he'd gleaned from his father's side of the family. With a black marker, he began drawing the chart that would eventually organize his relatives' traits into neat little boxes. It was too bad that his own problems couldn't be sorted out as easily.

Nana heard Jake shut his bedroom door and collapsed into the closest chair and whispered, "Oh, Elizabeth Jean, I miss you so much. I want to do what's best for Jake, but I don't know what that means anymore." She rested her head in her hands and cried softly so Jake wouldn't hear. She didn't notice as her tears formed perfect shallow-pooled orbs on her clean floor.

*   *   *

A shrill bark, more of a yip than anything, interrupted Jake's concentration. He was sitting on his bed playing a video game. Without even looking out the window, he knew it was the neighbor's dog, Honey. How could such a small dog's bark be so big? He pressed pause and looked around. His room was different but familiar at the same time. The different characters from *Toy Story* decorated his sheets. He recognized Buzz Lightyear, Woody, and Slinky Dog. *What the hell?* The walls of his room were painted a sky blue, and, on the ceiling, white, puffy clouds floated realistically.

He leapt from his bed and crossed the room to look in his mirror. He saw himself--only a much younger self. Jake realized he was dreaming, but everything was so vivid. Honey was still barking, but she faded into the background as another sound moved to the forefront. He willed himself to wake, but then he heard her. She was singing his goodnight song. He smiled; her voice was so sweet. She used to sing him to sleep every single night. As the melody reached his ears, he was instantly soothed. All the tension, fear, and anxiety left him as he gently swayed to the soothing cadence of his mother's voice, a sound he hadn't heard in the nine years since it was stolen from him.

The song was abruptly cut off. Jake listened carefully, tilting his head like a dog, but he heard nothing. Silence. Then Honey's high-pitched bark came once before it too was abruptly stopped. Silence. Jake's heart raced. Something wicked was there with him. He could sense its evil as apprehension settled into his every molecule. Slowly, gradually, a sound slithered stealthily up the stairs and through his bedroom door--a pounding, an ominous thumping that forced Jake to cover his ears. It bore into him, having a rhythm of its own, an awful tempo that mocked him in its unrelenting repetition. He screamed, but the sound was swallowed by malevolence.

Jake woke suddenly, gasping for air. His heart threatened to erupt from his chest, but he only heard the sound from his nightmare.

CHAPTER 5

"Do you want to come over to my house for supper tonight?" Amber asked Jake. "Mom's making her world-famous lasagna." The sky was turning a rosy pink as the sun began its slow descent to the horizon. They were walking hand in hand to Jake's ancient pickup truck in the school's nearly empty parking lot. Its original color was dark blue, but it was hard to tell with all the rust. Jake liked to joke that the rust was winning out.

"I can't tonight. I have to interview Nana and Papa about family stuff for my bio project," Jake stated dejectedly. Spending time with Amber sounded a lot more appealing than facing the past. He opened the passenger door for her, and she climbed inside.

Amber waited for Jake to get behind the steering wheel and said, "That's okay. Maybe we can do it later this week." When she realized what she'd said, she giggled and said quietly, "Have supper at my house, that is."

Jake looked over at her and raised his eyebrows. "Someone's sure got her mind in the gutter. What a perv," he added playfully. The truck awoke begrudgingly and lurched, rumbling noisily, toward the school's exit.

"I think that maybe I'm spending too much time with Ryan. His dirty mind must be contagious." Amber had spent the afternoon at Jake's cross-country meet. Ryan and Adam had been there as well, cheering on Jake in his 3.1 mile race through the woods behind the school. He'd finished second, only six seconds behind the first place finisher from Franklin Academy.   "I thought you two were actually starting to get along," Jake declared. "You seemed okay today. Maybe it was because you both had a common goal—to cheer on your hero."

Amber laughed. "Puh-lease! I didn't see Superman there. Now *you're* starting to sound as conceited as Ryan," she added as she poked his ribs playfully.

Jake faked a look of extreme disappointment and grabbed his chest. "You sure know how to insult a guy. Conceited as Ryan..." he muttered, "as if that's even possible."

Amber smiled at his theatrics. "If you truly wanted to act like Ryan, you would've invented some tale to explain why you didn't get first place today." She rushed ahead with her story. "Like maybe some Franklin Academy students ambushed you in the woods and attempted to tie you to a tree, but you gallantly fought them off ninja-style."

"That does sound like something he'd say," Jake stated thoughtfully. "We all know how he likes to make excuses—and he does like a good ninja story. But me? I don't have any excuses. That McCarthy kid is fast, but I do keep getting closer," Jake said happily. "Even though I'm sure he heard my constant wheezing, I think he was pretty surprised that I kept up until the very end."

"You were probably just distracted by my beauty at the finish line." Amber batted her eyelashes at Jake and winked.

"Now who sounds like Ryan, Ms. Cocky McBraggerson?" Jake made a left-hand turn at the stop sign as Amber gasped in mock horror.

"How dare you equate *me* to that giant turd!" she exclaimed.

"Turd? Did you just say turd?" Jake asked incredulously, a smile curling his lip.

"Yes. Yes, I did, and I will not apologize for it. My little sister says it constantly, so I decided to bring it back—just like skinny jeans, neon colors, and the side ponytail," she responded seriously.

One of the things Jake found most attractive about Amber was her sense of humor. She could be so serious about something so ridiculous. Jake thought she would be a great addition to the Saturday Night Live cast, but Amber had more lofty plans for her future—something to do with taking over the White House. "Amber, I'm glad that you can joke about Ryan even though he's a complete jackass to you."

"Jake, I'm a woman; therefore, I am more mature than your childish friend. I know he's going to be around a lot, so I've simply decided to take the bad with the good," Amber said sweetly taking Jake's free hand in hers. "And even though there's a whole lot of bad, I've devised a unique way to tune him out," she said seriously.

"You must be a genius. I bet you could make millions selling your new method to his teachers, parents, and to the entire female population of the school," Jake teased.

"Joke all you want. I just might do that and then laugh all the way to the bank," Amber replied as Jake pulled into her driveway.

63

"I don't think you need the money with that rich daddy of yours. Your house is almost as nice as Adam's father's." It was true. Amber's parents had totally renovated one of the oldest houses in town. It had three floors, not including the basement, which had been converted into a home gym.

"You know what else the Green and Krovlovski families have in common? My mom sleeps with the hired help too." She kissed Jake goodbye and jogged to the front door.

Jake laughed aloud as he carefully backed out of the driveway and waved to Amber's dad as he passed by on the riding lawnmower. As Jake neared his home, he yawned widely. After he was awakened from last night's nightmare, he'd tossed and turned for two hours. Eventually, at around three a.m., he'd dozed off but slept fitfully. Fatigue was making his eyelids heavy, so Jake rolled down his window and turned up the radio. He still needed to talk to his grandparents, and he knew that discussion was not going to be easy.

*   *   *

There's something obviously wrong with Justin, thought Adam. *Why am I the only one who sees it?* Adam watched from the kitchen window as Justin once again tried to kiss Sandy, the fourteen-year old blonde cheerleader whose bra size was definitely higher than her IQ. They were swimming in the heated pool, an eerie mist hovering over the warm water. She was clad in a skimpy bikini and looked as though she belonged on the cover of the *Sports Illustrated Swimsuit Edition.* She deftly swam away from Justin's attempts, and Adam

64

felt himself cheering on her escape. *Wow*, Adam thought sarcastically, *Justin's swimming lessons have really paid off.*

She'd arrived about twenty minutes ago, her blonde hair flying wildly behind her as she sped down their driveway on her four-wheeler. Although Sandy was breaking the law in so many ways, driving without a helmet and along a restricted road, this wasn't an unusual mode of transportation for teens in this small town. Since she lived only a half mile away, the chance of her getting caught was next to nil. He watched as Sandy now floated lazily on her back, and it was hard for Adam to equate this goddess with the redneck girl who had torn across their lawn on her all-terrain vehicle. He knew his father would be furious when he saw the tire tracks all over his pristine yard, but he also knew that his brother would not get into any trouble.

Adam knew Justin's plan, and it sickened him. All he wanted to do was have sex with Sandy, and she was too naïve (and too young and stupid) to know any better. She'd been over just about every night that week since her first "swimming lesson" on Saturday morning. Justin could be extremely charming when he wanted to be, but it was all just a show. *Why don't girls realize what he's after? Don't they warn each other?* Why did Adam feel as though he had to watch out for all of the girls his brother paraded in and out of the house?

Adam went into the living room, eating a plum as he went. He flopped down on the couch and turned on the television. He turned down the volume so he'd be able to hear the two lovebirds outside.

He figured he'd wander outdoors if he heard Sandy's high-pitched protests subside. *I wish we had some adult supervision around here,* Adam thought glumly. His father was always working late, and his stepmother, Julia, was probably off romancing Pasquel behind the rhododendron bush again.

Adam sighed in frustration. Now that he no longer had Gigi, it seemed that everyone he was supposed to look up to was a complete failure in the human being department. His stepmother was a cheating slut whom Adam had actually caught coming on to his older brother, Charles, last Christmas. Who knows what would have happened if Adam hadn't walked into the room. His mother was a drunk who'd abandoned him without a second glance. His father was a total shyster who'd step over an old lady's fallen body just to get at her purse. His brothers were sex-craved lunatics who would stop at nothing to win that stupid bet. Adam never talked to his brothers about their sex lives, but he had overheard Justin boasting to Charles over the phone that he'd slept with six girls in the last three months. What sickened Adam the most was the fact that he suspected their father knew about the bet and supported their "healthy competition."

Adam wandered back into the kitchen to wash the plum juice from his hands and face. It was getting dark quickly, and he could barely see the pool from the window over the sink. Even though warm water rushed over his hands, he went completely cold. He watched, sickened, as Justin wrapped Sandy in a passionate embrace. Justin fumbled with the ties on Sandy's bikini top, but she wriggled away and splashed him playfully. Adam smiled, glad to see her still playing hard to get. As he walked by the patio doors, he flipped on the outdoor lights. He didn't want Justin getting too cozy in the dark. Adam had started to get to know Sandy over the summer when she'd hung out with Amber, so he didn't want to see her getting hurt. This past week, though, she'd spent more time with Justin and no time with Amber, probably because she actually thought Justin really liked her. Little did she know that he'd stop talking to her completely after he added her to his "list."

Justin had been wooing her for almost a week and hadn't gotten anything in return. Adam chuckled to himself. He knew that his brother had put in too much time to simply drop her now. He silently prayed that she'd hold out indefinitely, but there had been other "nice" girls, and Adam knew that Justin had his ways. He frowned and concluded that Sandy would eventually succumb to Justin's sick whims. They all did. Adam just didn't know why.

*   *   *

Jake was in his room filling in the grid he had created for his project. He now had all the information about his great-grandparents and his grandparents. Some of the stories Nana had told about her parents had been quite interesting. He had never known that her parents were runners. Nana's parents had met while on the track team in high school. Her father had competed in the decathlon and had been quite successful. He had even broken records in the long jump and hurdles. "He used to do this one trick just for us kids," Nana recalled dreamily. "All of our friends would gather around, and he'd jump clear across the hood of his car. It was so amazing to see. We used to tell our friends that he could fly."

Jake's Grandfather Carver had also been a runner in college. He wasn't much of a jumper, but he ran the 5k and the mile. "I wasn't a star by any stretch of the imagination," he admitted, "but I was usually the second or third guy on our team. That's why I was so good at chasing you down when you were younger. Even as a toddler, you were pretty quick," he proudly added. Jake had decided that all of that running ancestry must have made it down the genetic line to him. He had the long, lean body of a runner and had tons of endurance.

Most of his relatives had brown hair, like him, but only Papa had his gray-blue eyes. Nana and her mother both had bright blue eyes. It was interesting to trace the dominant and recessive genes throughout the family tree he'd mapped out. It turned out that most of his family members had been college educated. He wondered if that meant they were intelligent or just driven.

Jake stared at the blanks in his chart. He needed information about his parents and then he'd be done. *That would be the hard part,* he decided. Once again, he shut himself into his closet, took out the small box from behind the secret door, and reverently traced the initials *E.J.D.* He slowly opened the wooden lid and shuffled through the five photographs until he found the one he was looking for. There was a small boy, about four years old, with two good-looking parents holding him aloft together. Everyone was smiling and happy, especially the little boy whose laughter was captured forever in this treasured photo. The young man and woman looked so happy with their only child.

Jake leaned his head back against the closet wall and closed his eyes, exhausted by the strength it took to forget all this time. He allowed his mind to travel back ten years. It had been a lazy Sunday afternoon. Jake had been in his room reading the comic book his father had bought him that morning when he'd gone out for muffins. He'd picked up all their favorites--chocolate chip for Jake, banana for his wife, Elizabeth, and lemon poppy for himself. Jake could remember every detail like a horror movie playing behind his eyelids. His memories caused a wake of emotions that left Jake shaking, huddled into the corner of his tiny closet still clutching the photograph.

Even now, he heard the arguing, which escalated into full-scale fury on his father's part. He heard drawers being pulled open and slammed shut. He heard his mother's calm tone be replaced by pleading sobs then crescendo into screams of terror. He had gone to the top of the staircase to investigate but was stopped short by the repetitive wet thumping he heard. He was petrified and unable to move until he heard an uncanny moaning from the kitchen. That sound had returned for years in all of his nightmares. It was a sound of desperation, hatred, and misery.

He ran to his parent's bedroom to dial 911. It seemed to take forever to crawl across the queen sized mattress to reach the phone resting on the nightstand between the wall and bed. He had barely told the operator his address when he heard heavy, thudding footsteps on the stairs. He scurried under the bed and watched his father's sensible brown shoes walk around to where Jake stood only seconds before. When his father's weight came crashing down, shaking the mattress violently, Jake almost yelped aloud in panic. He covered his mouth and squeezed his eyes tight.

Greg Carver, Jake's one-time hero had murdered his wife and now lay muttering on the bed. In an eerie, listless voice, his litany of questions bombarded Jake's eardrums. "What did I do? How did this happen? What do I do now?" Those unanswered questions rang out in an ever-increasing volume until Jake clapped his hands over his ears. Silent tears ran down his cheeks. Never had he been so afraid and confused. This was not his father; this was a stranger...a monster.

Suddenly, Greg moved and became silent all at once. His legs swung over the edge of the bed, and his feet thumped against the floor, spread wide. Jake removed his hands from his ears and listened carefully. Then, he too could hear the booming voices of the policemen below. Jake longed to call out, but that's when he saw the gleam of steel. The knife's point was aimed at the floor, dangling only inches away from Jake's face. An orb of thick, sticky, red-black liquid inched along the edges, gathered at the end, hovered for just an instant, and dropped to the floor, a perfect sphere marring the maple plank. Jake screamed until his breath was gone, and four policemen, guns drawn, entered the room, shouting. Jake scrambled out from underneath the other side of the bed, and a policeman whisked him away before he could witness his father slice his own throat.

*   *   *

Adam watched as the headlights of Sandy's four-wheeler cut a swath through the darkness. The mailbox at the end of the driveway was visible momentarily before Sandy turned onto the main road and sped toward her house. Everything was swallowed once again by icy shadows.

Julia had really come through tonight. Just when Adam thought he'd have to break up the soon-to-be R-rated events in the pool area, Julia had stumbled through the gate, drunk again, to find Justin kissing Sandy. Julia wasn't the least bit embarrassed, although Sandy was obviously mortified. She'd climbed quickly out of the pool and wrapped herself in a towel. Julia continued chatting away, completely unaware of Sandy's discomfort. Justin looked at Julia with hatred and disgust. Adam knew he would wait until Sandy was gone before he yelled at his stepmother for ruining his night. He wouldn't want Sandy to see his true colors. As soon as Sandy had pulled on her clothes over her wet bathing suit, Justin walked her out to the driveway. Adam, finally relieved of his guard duty, had climbed the stairs to his bedroom to watch Sandy drive away, safe for one more night.

He turned away from his window just in time to see an enraged Justin flying at him. He had no time to react.

Justin grabbed Adam by his shirt and slammed his back into the wall. "Why the hell were you spying on us? Did you think I couldn't see you watching out the kitchen window? Is that what it takes to get you off?" Still clinging to his tee shirt, he spun Adam away from the wall and flung him across the room like he was a piece of trash.

Adam fell over his desk chair and landed in a heap on the floor. He scrambled to his feet before Justin could kick him. He had learned from past fights not to lie, prone to attack, on the floor. A year ago Justin had cracked two of his ribs, but he hadn't told his father the whole truth. Justin had concocted a tale about a wrestling match, and his father had believed every word. Adam hadn't bothered to contradict his story since Justin had threatened him, and he doubted whether his father would even believe him. He knew brothers fought, but this wasn't normal. Justin was an unpredictable storm, one that ravaged everything in its path and then simply moved on. His rage could be turned on and off like a light switch.

"You perverted little cock-block," Justin hissed. Hatred fueled him, poison coated his words, and his eyes shone with a glint of steel.

Adam inched backward toward his bedroom door, gauging the distance and wondering if he could escape downstairs before Justin caught him. He knew better than to speak. Silence was his defense. Words would only add fuel to Justin's fury.

Justin took a step closer to Adam, closing the gap. A smile curled his lips when he saw the sheer terror in his brother's eyes. He reached out quickly and grabbed Adam's shirt again and pulled him in close. "Let me give you some advice," he growled. "Stop acting like a little homo and maybe you'll be able to get your own piece of ass." He slapped Adam lightly on the cheek. "If I catch you watching me again, I won't be so nice." He shoved him away and strode out of the room.

Adam shook in fear and anger. *I'm perverted?* he seethed. *I'm not the one trying to screw a fourteen-year-old.* After closing and locking his bedroom door, Adam peered into the mirror hanging above his dresser. His cheek was only slightly red where Justin had slapped him. That's what confused Adam the most. How could Justin appear so erratic one moment but have the sense not to leave a mark on his brother's face? Adam, suddenly exhausted, flopped onto his bed, his appetite for dinner totally gone.

*   *   *

The wind picked up suddenly, and the autumn leaves cartwheeled around the young couple's ankles. They walked hand in hand along the trail that twisted along the gorge's edge. Amber's hair blew wildly, so she deftly pulled it back into a ponytail. She always wore a hair band around her wrist for such an occasion. "What did you want to tell me, Jake?" she asked. She looked up to meet his eyes. She was tall for a girl, but Jake still had four inches on her.

"I just wanted to bring you here so you could enjoy the view. Isn't it pretty with all the changing colors?" Some of the trees had begun to lose their leaves, but the majority still wore their autumn's best. The vibrant reds, yellows, and oranges were amazing.

Amber stood quietly, listening to the leaves whisper their secrets to the wind. Jake stood behind her and wrapped his arms protectively around her. "Can you believe we were swimming here just a week ago?" Amber asked. "I'll never understand the weather here."

"Don't worry. No one does. Wait until you have to suffer through a North Country winter," Jake replied.

"Have you forgotten, Jake, that I'm from the Snow Belt? I'm no wussy, you know. I think I can handle it," Amber said smiling. The crunch of leaves sounded beneath their feet, joining their conversation noisily.

"I know. You get a lot of snow in Syracuse, but wait until it hits forty below zero, then we'll see who's a wuss. Follow me; I want you to see how pretty the water looks falling over the waterfall. We're here at the perfect time of day, so we'll see little rainbows in the spray."

Jake took Amber's hand to help her over two giant boulders that blocked the way. There was no path on this side of the gorge, and the two continued cautiously over the rough terrain. After fifteen minutes of difficult climbing, the pair stood atop the waterfall. "This was so worth it," Amber gushed, perspiration making her face glisten. "This is totally incredible, Jake."

Jake pulled Amber close against his body, her eyes closed as she anticipated a kiss. Jake gently brushed away some wisps of hair from her face and shoved her off the edge. Her eyes opened in horror, and Jake watched, captivated, as Amber's arms flailed wildly, searching for a hold that would never materialize. Just as her body collided on the sharp rocks below, Jake awoke and sat up like a bolt of lightning. The sheets were twisted around his legs, and his blanket lay pooled on the floor beside his narrow bed. The sheets were damp with his sweat. *It was just a nightmare. I would never hurt Amber,* he reassured himself. *I am not my father.*

CHAPTER 6

Jake and Amber had spent the day watching a horror movie marathon with Amber's father. Ben Green was a movie buff, especially when it came to old slasher flicks. He'd even converted part of the third level into a home theater, complete with a popcorn machine. Much to the disappointment of her father, Amber had laughed uncontrollably during the bloodiest scenes. She called Freddy Kruegar a hack with poor fashion sense and Jason Voorhees a loser with mommy issues.

"Jesus, Amber, you're really ruining these movies for me," Ben grumbled as he ejected the DVD.

"Dad, I've told you a million times these movies just aren't scary," Amber teased. They're too old, the special effects suck, and everything is sooooo predictable." She held up a finger, took a deep breath, barked, "Action" and clapped her hands together. In slow-motion, she began to run across the room. Looking over her shoulder, she cried out, "Oh, my, a deadly supernatural killer is after me. I guess I should be tripping on a non-existent tree root now." She dropped to the carpet and clutched her ankle. Ben and Jake looked on, amused. "Even though I just ran a mile through the woods while the murderer walked very slowly, he should be here momentarily to kill me." She leapt gracefully to her feet and took a bow. "Do you see the ridiculousness of it now?"

"Wow, you're a horrible actress," Ben quipped. He turned to Jake, hoping to find an ally. "What did you think, Jake—the movies were terrifying, right?"

"Well," he glanced back and forth between Amber and her father. Amber's hands were placed firmly on her hips, and Ben's eyes pleaded with him to agree. Jake wasn't sure whose side he should take. "Um...I think," he began nervously as they both stared at him eagerly. "I think I hear Mrs. Green calling us for dinner."

"You gutless wonder!" Amber laughed as she hurled a throw pillow at his head.

Jake hadn't truly been watching the movies. When blood and gore ruled the TV screen, he always took his mind on vacation and allowed his brain to wander aimlessly through more pleasing images—Amber's smile, Nana baking, Ryan and Adam fighting like brothers. This time, however, it was impossible to erase the remnants of last evening's nightmare. Over and over, the scene played out in his brain. He could still see the shock in Amber's eyes, her arms windmilling blindly, her crumpled body on the rocks. The memory was a cancer spreading throughout every cell in his body. *Am I poisoned?* he wondered.

Jake used the side of his fork to snowplow Patsy Green's homemade macaroni and cheese into two separate piles on his plate. Amber shot him a glance and raised a questioning eyebrow at him. Sheepishly, he took a bite. Amber could tell something was wrong. Normally, Jake ate more than her two sisters combined, but he hadn't even finished his first serving. She plopped her napkin beside her plate. "Let's go for a walk," Amber insisted. She could tell Jake was preoccupied with something, and she was certain he would never talk about it where her parents could overhear.

They walked slowly, hand in hand, out to the backyard. No one spoke. Amber led Jake to the hammock and sat down. She patted the place beside her, and Jake took a seat. "I was so happy when dad put this up," Amber rambled, needing to break the silence. "It's more comfortable than my bed, and it's a lot quieter here than inside the house where Caitlyn and Lauryn are either arguing or making up dance routines or arguing *while* making up dance routines." Jake's silence made her nervous. She bit her lip to stop babbling. "Here, lay down beside me and we'll wait for the stars," she suggested as she stretched out.

The hammock was big enough for the two to lie side by side so they could stare into the giant elm tree's canopy of leaves. Jake swung one of his long legs hung over the side so he could gently rock them. "This is pretty nice," Jake conceded. The night was chilly. They both wore sweatshirts and jeans to ward off the fall wind's bite.

Amber turned toward Jake and rested her head against his chest. She lightly traced his lips with her fingertip. "You've been really quiet all day. Normally you laugh at all of my stupid jokes, and, not to brag or anything, but I was especially funny today. So, what's up?" Amber asked lightly as she took his hand. A pause, pregnant with Jake's uneasiness, met Amber's question.

Jake blew out a long breath as though he'd just surfaced from a deep dive. "I want to tell you," he replied hesitantly, "but…" He trailed off as glimpses of last night's horrifying dream flashed through his mind.

Amber waited patiently, lightly rubbing the back of Jake's hand with her thumb. She knew with certainty that Jake would speak—that he would eventually reveal the source of his reticence.

Jake opened his mouth to talk, but nothing came out. He'd spent his life hiding the truth, and now, when he wanted to reveal himself, he wasn't sure what to even say.

He cleared his throat nervously and tried again. "I've been wondering all day if I should tell you this," he started slowly, "but I just don't know where to start. It's something I've never told anyone before." Jake was glad for the darkness; it hid all the physical signs of his torment. However, he couldn't hide the agony in his voice.

"Ryan and Adam don't even know?" Amber asked.

"No. I've never told a single person. That's why it's so hard to do now. I knew I'd have to tell someone someday, but this biology assignment really got me thinking and sort of sped up my plans." The North Star was visible just to the left, and Jake made a wish. It was automatic, a simple plea made a million times before, but he knew it was useless. He'd *always* known it to be impossible to wish back the dead, but he'd never stopped begging, even after ten years. He sighed loudly. "I've had to face my past, and I guess I've started to worry about things too. I need to talk to someone about it before my brain explodes."

Amber sat up on her elbow and stared into his eyes. "What is it? You can tell me, Jake." She couldn't even begin to imagine a secret big enough to hide from his two best friends.

A strand of her blond hair swung across her face, and Jake tucked it gently behind her ear. "Let's walk," he said simply. "I feel really jumpy all the sudden." They began to cross the wide expanse of lawn, the floodlights attached to the house their only source of light.

Amber didn't speak. She didn't want to push him. Instead, she took his hand in hers. That small gesture of tenderness propelled Jake forward. "Do you know why I live with my grandparents?" he asked.

"Yes," she stated sheepishly. "I asked Adam. Your parents died when you were seven," she replied evenly. "He told me it was a car accident."

"Yeah, well, that's what everyone thinks. That's what I tell anyone brave enough to ask. Not many do. I guess they assume or just ask someone else if they're interested," Jake said, embarrassed by his dishonesty. "It's actually so much worse." He suddenly let go of Amber's hand and rubbed his now sweaty palms onto his jeans.

Amber stopped and pulled Jake toward her so she could look into his eyes. "You
don't need to be ashamed of what happened to your parents, Jake. You can tell me the truth. I won't run away screaming; I promise."

Jake studied Amber's open face in the yellow glow of the garage lights. He thought he had memorized this face and all of its

80

expressions, but he had never seen this combination of naked emotion before. He saw worry, curiosity, and a hint of fear. He knew she cared deeply about him. He knew that he could trust her with his darkest secret, but he couldn't look at her as he struggled to find the right words. When he did, they flew from between his lips. "Actually, my father stabbed my mother to death and then killed himself with the same knife when the police arrived," Jake revealed in one hurried breath. All at once he felt some relief in telling the truth.

"Oh my God." Amber's voice quavered. She hugged Jake to her tightly.

He swallowed hard and made eye contact once again. "Can't you see why I couldn't tell anyone? It's just so messed up." Jake's voice cracked with those last words.

Silence settled over them like a blanket as Amber processed Jake's horrible story. They wandered across the yard. Shadows drew closer as they neared the winding brook behind the house. Its gurgling broke the quiet, a lighthearted melody that couldn't penetrate Amber's whirling thoughts. This was bigger than she could have imagined. Minutes passed as she fought to find the right words. "It *is* awful, Jake, but you can't change anything. *You* didn't do anything wrong."

"But that's what's worrying me now. I mean," Jake licked his lips nervously and ran his fingers through his hair, "violent behavior can be inherited. This is the kind of stuff we're learning about in biology right now."

Amber couldn't hide her anger. She stopped abruptly and faced Jake. Darkness masked their features. "That's ridiculous, Jake," Amber chided.

"But, how do I really *know* that I won't do the same thing?" Jake asked miserably, turning away.

"Oh, Jake." Compassion bloomed in Amber's heart. "You can't take on your father's guilt. It's his and his alone. You can't let his crime be your burden." She spoke calmly and with resolution. "I've only known you for a few months, but I know with certainty that you are kind, thoughtful, and gentle. I've never seen you do or say anything even remotely cruel. You're an absolute sweetheart. You *couldn't* hurt anyone," she emphasized reassuringly.

Jake cleared his throat. "That's what bothers me. I don't remember my father ever doing anything mean. He didn't yell at me or spank me or beat my mother. He didn't have a drinking problem or use drugs. There's no explanation for his behavior. He just snapped. How do I know I won't do the same thing? I don't even know what they were arguing about that day," Jake confessed despondently.

Amber turned quickly to face him. "You were there when your father...when it happened?" Amber asked incredulously. "You didn't see it happen, did you?" Amber was shocked at this bit of news and couldn't hold her curiosity at bay.

His voice shook slightly as he spoke. "I was in my room reading, but even though I didn't see anything, I heard things. I knew what was happening even at the age of seven."

Amber had stopped walking, frozen by Jake's words. "Holy shit," she whispered. How could Jake be so normal? She pictured a small boy with pale blue eyes filled with sorrow. Swallowing the lump in her throat, she embraced him, feeling his hot cheek against her cold one.

Jake, however, felt nothing. All he could hear was his father's wail of despair and a rhythmic sodden pounding.

*   *   *

Sandy awoke in Justin Krovlovski's bed. She looked around the cluttered, dimly lit room, completely confused. She felt lightheaded and lethargic. When she sat up, a wave of dizziness washed over her, and her head throbbed violently. She swung her legs over the bed and slowly stood up. With each movement, her brain felt as though it would explode. "Justin?" she called out softly. There was no response. She fumbled for the clock beside the bed, having to move aside two magazines and a dirty glass in the process. Her vision was slightly fuzzy, but the bright digital numbers practically screamed the time. It was 10:13 at night. *Oh, my God. My parents are going to kill me,* Sandy thought as she hurriedly moved to the door, adjusting her shorts unconsciously.

Sandy raced through the giant house but encountered no one. The downstairs was dark, the kitchen lit only by a dim nightlight. Her shadow chased her as she passed through the front door. Earlier that day, she had parked her four-wheeler near the garage, and as she jogged toward it, she was suddenly overcome by nausea. She stopped quickly and threw up. Her headache was worsening, but all

83

she could think about was the trouble she was going to be in when she got home. When she started the ATV, its deafening roar threatened to split open her throbbing skull. She sped down the driveway and turned quickly onto the shoulder of the road. The knobby tires tossed up loose gravel that pinged against the undercarriage. *What am I going to tell them? They've probably called the cops already.* Sandy tried to think of a reasonable explanation, but her brain just wouldn't work properly.

Sandy arrived at her house just a few moments later. She expected to see flashing police cars parked on her lawn. Instead, she saw only a dark house. Relieved, Sandy entered the house and found a note on the kitchen table. ***Your father and I went out to eat and to the movies. Will be home by 11.*** Sandy, feeling calm now that she had avoided a catastrophic grounding, headed to her room.

She took two Tylenol and slumped into her desk chair. Now, bewilderment set in. The last thing she remembered was eating lunch with Justin. He had been so romantic, setting up a picnic beside the pool. He had even brought out some wine in two fancy crystal glasses. *Was it the wine?* Sandy had had only had the occasional sips from her father's beer, and once she'd had some champagne at a wedding. *I only remember drinking half the glass,* Sandy thought frowning. She had never heard of anyone passing out on so little alcohol. *But if I were sick, why would Justin just leave me like that?* Feeling angry now, Sandy decided to take a shower. She vowed that she would confront him in the morning, and she wouldn't let him sweet-talk his way out of this one.

She walked into the bathroom and turned on the water, then turned to look at herself in the mirror. She looked different somehow. It was her eyes, she realized. Her pupils were huge, the blackness of them almost completely dominating the blue of her irises. She stared until the steam from the shower fogged the mirror.

She turned away and began undressing. She noticed that her shirt was on backwards. *That's weird,* she thought. It wasn't until she was completely undressed that comprehension set in. She now knew what had happened. She crumpled to her knees onto the fluffy white bathmat. Disappointment and shame consumed her completely. *How could he?* she dared to ask herself. She laid down, her face now against the cool linoleum. She slowly curled into a fetal position and drew in ragged breaths. Tears rolled across her cheeks and pooled on the green flooring. Her pile of clothes was mere inches from her face, her torn and bloody panties atop the heap, a sad symbol of robbed innocence.

*   *   *

Adam had been checking the pool skimmer for frogs and other vermin when he heard the kitchen door slam. He was alarmed because no one should have been home. He crept silently but quickly around the garage and was shocked to see Sandy retching in the driveway. She was standing in the pool of light cast by one of the motion detectors on the garage. He was about to call her name when he stopped. As her four-wheeler raced down the driveway, Adam was haunted by what he'd seen. He'd seen it before, and he had hoped he'd never see it again. Last spring, Adam had been watching movies late into the evening and was heading to bed when he saw a girl leave Justin's room. She was crying hysterically and attempting to correct her shirt that was inside out. When she saw Adam in the hall, she'd whimpered and started running down the stairs. When Adam looked in Justin's room, Justin had said simply and with a lecherous grin, "I guess she had regrets."

Adam focused back into the present and watched as Sandy skidded onto the road. He couldn't escape the image burned into his brain. Right before Sandy had climbed onto her four-wheeler, Adam had seen that her shirt was on backwards.

*   *   *

Sandy's private turmoil was interrupted with sounds of normalcy when her parents returned ten minutes later. Sandy could hear her parents whispering in the kitchen, her mother's unique but rarely heard giggle, and finally the creaking of the old oak stairs. She heard her bedroom door open softly. Sandy faced the opposite wall, clutching her tear soaked pillow and feigning sleep. The hall light threw a rectangle on the wall. She watched as the rectangle of light from the hallway disappeared with the closing of her door. She shuddered visibly when she heard the click of the door. It was an audible symbol marking the end of something.

Sandy had taken a hot shower in an attempt to rid herself of the humiliation she felt. She had hidden all evidence that proved this night had actually occurred. A plastic grocery bag holding the clothes she'd worn that day was now shoved underneath her bookcase. She planned on burning the clothes in the morning when her parents made the usual Sunday visit to grandma in the nursing home.

Sandy felt restless. She knew that she'd never be able to sleep. Guilt and self-loathing overwhelmed her. She kicked off the covers and made her way to her closet. She quietly opened the door and reached for the journal she kept hidden in a shoebox. She carried the red leather-bound book to her bed and turned on the small reading lamp clipped to her headboard. She began writing, pushing so hard with her pen that the pages threatened to tear.

What happened today? I'm missing at least eight hours of memory. I don't remember anything. How can that be? Did I really just have sex for the first time? I think Justin took advantage of me. That's why he gave me wine, but what if there was something in the wine? There must be an explanation. I thought he really liked me, but I guess I should have listened to Steph. She told me that he was way out of my league, but I just thought she was jealous because he dumped her for me. Listen to how ridiculous I sound!

What am I going to do now? I can't tell my parents. I can't tell Amber. I'm too ashamed and embarrassed. They'll totally hate me and think I'm a slut. What do I do when I see Justin at school? How can I face him? Will he even talk to me? Will he explain what happened? What if I get pregnant?

I thought he liked me, but how can I be so stupid? How could I ever believe that Justin Krovlovski would be interested in me? He's a senior; I'm a freshman. It's no wonder he did what he did. I was too stupid to know what he was after. I can't believe I thought he actually liked me!

Sandy threw her pen across the room in anger. She looked at the words scrawled in her journal. The writing was unrecognizable. Her usually flowery, cursive writing was replaced by angry slashes of ink in bold print. She closed her journal with a snap and returned it to its hiding place. *I hope this is all a nightmare, and when I wake up in the morning, it will only be a memory.* She curled onto her side. Her head throbbed dully, but the pain was subsiding.

* * *

Adam found what he was looking for in Justin's sock drawer. Next to a fake ID and a small baggie of marijuana, he discovered a vial of pills. Adam's suspicions were confirmed with a quick check on the Internet. Adam studied the picture on the computer screen and compared it to the pills spilled on the desk before him. There was no mistaking it; Justin was indeed using Rohypnol, a date rape drug, in order to surpass Charles's sexual record.

Adam felt as though he'd been punched in the stomach. How could his brother do such a thing? He knew Justin was downright vicious at times, but he didn't think he'd stoop to this level of evil. As Adam sat staring at the computer screen, however, he realized that deep down he *knew* his brother was capable of such a horrendous act. That's why he'd snooped around his room. He knew he'd find something awful.

All of a sudden, Adam thought about Sandy. *She must be so scared*, he thought. *Does she even know what he did to her?* Adam contemplated what he should do with his newfound knowledge. Should he tell his father? Would his father even care? He might

88

consider the legal consequences or how this ordeal might tarnish his reputation, but would he really be concerned about the welfare of God knows how many girls? It was then that Adam realized he was nothing like his family, and he felt relief in that insight.

Adam knew he had to do something. He couldn't let his brother continue raping these girls. Did he have the guts to go to the cops to rat out his own brother? He thought he did, but he couldn't help but wonder what Justin would do to him. How badly would Justin hurt him for this "betrayal?" What would his father think? Would Adam be ostracized for bringing shame upon the household? Did he really care?

CHAPTER 7

He jerked awake and sat up quickly, the narrow mattress still quaking from his sudden reaction. His heart pounded in his chest. He'd had the dream again. It was a good dream, not one of the many nightmares that still plagued his sleep. This dream was filled with light, laughter, and affection. He rarely dreamed of the two of them anymore, a beautiful woman and a young boy. He knew their names, but he dared not say them aloud, afraid that he might lose this peaceful moment. He lay back down on his bed and closed his eyes in an attempt to recapture the moment before he would, once again, be consumed by darkness.

It was a warm afternoon in summer, and the smell of wildflowers floated on a soothing breeze. The sun shone intensely through the leaves of the nearby elm trees, throwing dappled shadows across a green and yellow plaid picnic blanket. Two plastic wine glasses, half empty, sat atop the overturned picnic basket, which now served as a makeshift table. A plate of cheese, crackers, and sliced apples rested between the man and woman. She raised up her glass, the sun turning the wine a blood-red, and toasted him. A silent laugh shook her shoulders. The woman smiled at him as she spoke. He couldn't make out the words, only her playful mood.

The boy was close, running barefoot through the long grass next to a shallow stream. The woman pointed at the boy, amused. He looked over his shoulder to see the child chasing a monarch butterfly. He felt his own smile stretch across his face. He felt the woman's hand on his and turned toward her. Their lips met with the precision of long-acquainted lovers. The boy ran to them, momentarily forgetting the butterfly. He was anxious to share their attention and was instantly swallowed up by their affections.

The man opened his eyes and was met by the accusing glare of the concrete wall before him. He was glad for the opportunity to remember something good. Usually his dreams and memories ended in oceans of crimson. He went to the sink and splashed cold water onto his face. He looked into the mirror and saw the ugly raised scar that was a daily reminder of his torment. "What do you think of me?" he whispered to his reflection.

He turned back toward his bed and sank heavily down upon it. White spots danced around the edges of his vision. He closed his eyes tightly against the sudden searing pain and tried, without success, to regain a foothold into his sunny dreamworld—back to the before time—back to before he'd fallen off the precipice and into the inferno called rage.

CHAPTER 8

"How's the biology project coming along?" Amber asked Jake over the phone. Jake didn't answer right away, and Amber nervously began pacing her bedroom, angry at herself for bringing up such a sore subject so early in the morning. It was eight a.m., and Amber was hoping to go for a long walk with Jake. She hadn't wanted to push him further last night after he'd told her about his parents' deaths. It had been difficult for him just to reveal the facts, but she was worried about his genuine concern for his own future and whether or not he'd turn out like his father.

She was about to apologize when Jake said, "After I got home from your house last night, I started filling out my mom's section of the chart, but I still need some more information from Nana. I can't remember her height because I was little. She seemed so tall to me. Then I began to realize there are some other things I can't remember about her. Do you think that's bad?" Jake asked sadly. "I don't remember her eye color or her favorite food. Shouldn't I know this stuff?"

Amber could hear the frustration in his voice. She knew he was close to tears. "Jake, you were only seven when she died. Most seven year olds don't know their mother's eye color. They're too busy playing and having fun. I think you're being too hard on yourself. Have you ever talked to your grandparents about these things?" Amber asked.

"No," he replied quickly. "They rarely talk about Mom, and they *never* mention my father. It's like he never existed. I don't feel comfortable talking to them about what happened because Mom was their only daughter, and I always think that the mere mention of her name will make them sad. Does that make sense?" Jake was beginning to realize that they'd all been trying to forget about what had happened. In the process, however, they'd all been losing Elizabeth by ignoring their memories of her.

"You know what, Jake? I think your grandparents might be thinking the same thing. Maybe they don't talk about her because they're afraid you'll be sad. This project could actually be a good thing because it could get you guys talking about your mom again. And, you all need to realize that it's okay to feel sad. You miss your mom; your grandparents miss their daughter. That's normal, but you should be remembering her and talking about the great things she did. I bet Nana has some funny stories about her only daughter that would have you laughing your ass off. I bet she was a crazy kid." Amber flopped onto her bed and rolled onto her back. She hoped that she was giving the right advice.

"Amber, I think you should become a shrink and maybe have your own talk show."

Amber laughed, relieved that Jake hadn't been put off by her directness. "Don't suck up to me yet, Mr. Carver. The bill is in the mail, and I charge exorbitant prices for my sessions."

"You might just be worth the high cost. I guess I'll sit down with Nana and Papa after breakfast and sort of ease into a

93

conversation about Mom. Hopefully, they'll be able to fill in the blanks for me without getting upset." Amber had made it sound like such an easy thing to do. He could understand the logic in what she'd said, but he was still hesitant to unearth the topic that had been buried for so long.

"That sounds like a good idea. I wish you luck," she said brightly. "We're still going out later, right? If you change your mind, though, that's totally fine with me. We can watch TV at my house, do laundry, or even clean up all the cow crap in your barn. What do you say?" Amber asked hopefully.

"Although all those options sound fabulous, especially the one about cleaning up shit, I'd have to say that we are still going to Ryan's Halloween party tonight."

"Oh, all right then." Amber sighed loudly then stifled a giggle. She loved giving Jake a hard time for being friends with Ryan.

"Try to sound at least a little excited," Jake declared. Even though no one else dresses up anymore, I was thinking you could dress up as a sexy witch or something. How about it?"

"That sounds like a wonderful time," drawled Amber sarcastically. "I'd have to punch Ryan every time he asked me where my costume was, and I'd have to use my broom to ward off Adam. Jeez, can't you find that boy a girlfriend so he'll leave me alone?"

Jake laughed. He loved Amber's wit and the fact that she didn't see herself as the beauty she truly was. Everyone liked her because she was nice to everyone. Well, she wasn't nice to Ryan, but he deserved it. "I'll pick you up at five. We won't stay too long."

94

Jake began to imitate Nana's voice. "You don't need to be out all night, young lady. It's a school night, and I'm sure you have schoolwork to do."

Amber chuckled and said, "If you don't make it as a pharmacist, you could always become a transvestite. You have a lovely lady's voice, you know," she said in a deliciously deep, sexy voice.

When Amber hung up the phone, she thought about how perfect Jake was for her. She reached into her closet and pulled out a pair of sneakers and pulled them on, not bothering to untie the laces first. She was glad that Jake had decided to talk to his grandparents. She ran downstairs, grabbed the leash and her cocker spaniel Spencer, and went for a walk with the other important man in her life.

*   *   *

"Holy shit, Amber!" Ryan screamed a half second after he opened the door. One hand clutched his heart dramatically while the other clung to the door frame. "Please, take off the mask before I have a heart attack," Ryan gasped.

"Oh, my aching ass, Ryan! Is that the best you've got?" Amber replied as she shoved him out of her way. "I was expecting something a little less fourth grade, but what was I thinking? That's your mentality, right?" She walked past Ryan, cuffing the side of his head gently.

Jake watched Amber join the others in the living room and smiled. He couldn't believe his luck. She had it all...beauty, a killer body, brains, and a fiery personality. He walked past his flustered host and into the house. "Ryan, why don't you just give up? You'll never win; you're just too dumb." He winked at Ryan and also gave him a playful slap on the back of his head.

Ryan couldn't retaliate when a girl hit him, but he wasn't about to let the human toothpick get away with it. After all, he had a reputation to uphold, and besides…girls were there, and he felt their eyes watching. "That's it; you're dead," Ryan growled. He jumped on Jake's back. Jake's legs buckled, and the two tumbled to the floor.

Jake could tell by the surprised looks on the other guests' faces that they weren't one hundred percent sure that Ryan wasn't just fooling around. Their eyes and mouths were wide open. They didn't know Ryan like Jake did. Ryan, for all his swagger and big talk, was just a big softie. Jake began to laugh hysterically as Ryan put him in a head lock.

"Say it! Say it!" Ryan yelled as he tightened his hold. A grin danced at his lips, and the others relaxed, now knowing that this was all a game.

"Don't give up, babe," Amber cried out with fake desperation in her voice. "Don't let him take you alive," she shrieked. She threw a hand over her forehead and "fainted" onto the couch.

"Say it! Say Ryan Chapin is the best. Say it!"

Jake had been fighting against Ryan's hold when he suddenly stopped struggling. "Wow, someone's been working out," he said appreciatively wagging his eyebrows. In his best stereotypical gay man's lisp, he added, "And apparently that someone's into recreating scenes from *Brokeback Mountain!*"

Ryan threw Jake away from him. "Shut your ball washer! Jesus Christ, there are chicks here," Ryan hissed, looking around quickly to gauge his female guests' reactions. When Jake winked at him, Ryan chucked a pillow at Jake's head. "My God...you're so totally gay. No wonder the dyke has the hots for you."

Ten minutes later, the party had settled down. Everyone was casually flopped on the furniture watching *Halloween*. Amber and Jake sat on one end of the couch, holding hands. Adam sat at the other end, alone and deep in thought. Amber nudged him. "Why are you so quiet tonight, Adam? You didn't even join in on the festivities of the wrestling match."

"I have a lot on my mind, I guess," Adam replied quietly. "Did you talk to Sandy today? I thought she was coming to the party?"

"Oh, that's why you're so quiet," Amber teased. "Do you have a thing for Sandy now?"

"No," Adam replied a little too quickly, "I was just wondering, that's all."

"Ok, Adam." Amber winked. "I guess you'll have to wait until school on Monday to see her. She told me she was feeling sick so she didn't feel like coming."

Adam's stomach churned. He still hadn't decided what to do about Justin and Sandy. He knew he had to do something. The guilt was eating him alive. Adam wanted to help, but he didn't know how. What would she think of him if she knew that he had been home that night and had seen her leave? Worse yet, would she think that he knew all along and hadn't come to her rescue? Adam ignored the screams coming from the television; he had different nightmares running through his mind.

*   *   *

Jake and Amber were sitting in Jake's pickup, the noisy grumbling of the engine the only sound as they sat kissing in the driveway at Amber's house. It wasn't the most romantic background noise, Jake realized, but they needed the heat, for the night's chill announced winter's ominous approach. On the other hand, Jake was feeling a little too hot at the moment. To Jake, Amber's lips tasted like heaven, danger, and longing all rolled together. He was the one to break away first. "Aren't your parents going to wonder why we're sitting here?" he whispered. It was hard for him to concentrate. Their make-out sessions were getting longer and more intense, and Jake lacked the experience and the guts to take it much further. He leaned toward Amber and gently pressed his forehead against hers. "I don't really want to meet the end of your dad's baseball bat."

Amber leaned away from Jake and murmured, "You're such a drama queen. As if he'd ever take a bat to you. He likes you, you know." She took Jake's hand, shook it solemnly and said, "Thank you for the wonderful evening, Mr. Carver. I had a delightful time, good sir. I pray you make it back to your village unscathed astride your trusty steed. Fare thee well. I shall see thee on the morrow." She opened the door and gracefully jumped down from the truck. Turning, she said, "Honestly, Jake, my dad doesn't even like baseball. He'd be more likely to use a croquet mallet." Jake laughed and watched her jog to the front door and disappear inside.

Ten minutes later, Jake was climbing the creaky stairs to his room. His grandparents were already asleep, even though it was only 9:30. When he swung open his bedroom door, he was confronted by his biology project. The incomplete squares next to his mother's name screamed a silent accusation. *How could you have forgotten your own mother?* Jake picked up the piece of poster board and placed it face down on his desk.

After Jake's phone call with Amber that morning, he had approached the stove where his grandmother was busily piling scrambled eggs onto a plate. He stood beside her, set his hand on her shoulder and quietly asked, "Nana, do you think we could talk about mom after breakfast with Papa so I can add her information to my project?"

She had turned so quickly that some of the eggs spilled back into the frying pan. "Oh, my," she muttered as she quickly scooped up the spill. "I'm getting klutzy in my old age. Here, honey, why don't you bring these to the table?"

Jake looked closely at her as she handed him the platter. He knew what she was trying to do. After all, he'd been doing the same thing for years. She wanted to avoid the topic. She didn't want to remember. Jake felt instantly guilty for making his grandmother upset. He couldn't miss the tremor of her hands or how her face had paled at his question. He set the eggs on the recently polished table. He was about to forget the whole thing when Amber's words came back to him. He turned back to Nana and whispered softly, "This doesn't need to be sad. I just want you to remember all the good things about her." He'd left it at that, afraid to upset her further. After a quick and very silent breakfast, he'd spent the next few hours helping his grandfather fix the ancient tractor.

Had that only been this morning? It felt so long ago. He pulled down the window shades and turned to his bed. He spotted a book lying on his pillow. He sat on his unmade bed and opened it. It was a scrapbook, and inside were all of his mother's achievements. He flipped quickly through the pictures, certificates, and ribbons. He had never seen this scrapbook, but then again, he was never much of a snooper. His grandmother must have stored it away just as he had stored away his precious few memories in his mother's jewelry box. Jake realized that his Nana had left this for him. Maybe she was getting ready to face the past as well. He wondered how often Nana paged through this book to remember her only child, and Jake thought back to all the times he'd sat alone in his closet crying softly while he lovingly caressed the few photos he had of his once-happy family. Why did they each suffer alone? Why couldn't they share this sorrow? Amber was right. They needed to talk about his mother in order to keep her memory alive.

Jake spent the next few hours mesmerized by the red leather bound scrapbook that revealed so much about his mother. His fingers traced the embossed gold star on her kindergarten graduation certificate, drifted over her first and second place gymnastics ribbons, touched her face in each photograph, trailed through the red and black strings of her high school graduation tassel, and finally rested on a Def Leppard concert stub dated September 14, 1986 and labeled *First Date with Greg Carver*. Jake longed to tear out that last memento, hoping to eradicate the past, but he realized with resignation that he couldn't delete the past without erasing himself and every memory he had of his mother.

He placed the scrapbook on his desk and grabbed the black permanent marker from the floor beside the poster board. He began to fill in almost all of the squares beside his mother's name. After only a few minutes, Jake sat back and looked at the project that had forced him to face his gruesome family secret. He had managed to bury his past for ten years, but he was beginning to think that facing it head on might actually have a positive impact, not only on his life, but on his grandparent's lives as well. He turned out the light, stripped to his underwear, and climbed under his covers. He slept deeply and dreamed of a young, leotard-clad girl performing perfect cartwheels.

CHAPTER 9

The final bell had rung, and the usual mass chaos ensued in the hallways. Adam slammed shut his locker. He had just seen his brother with the new girl. Justin's arm was casually draped over her shoulders, and she was laughing at whatever he had said. Adam didn't know a lot about this girl…only that her name was Michele, she'd moved from Minnesota, she'd enrolled yesterday, and she was a tenth grader.

New students were considered curiosities at most small schools, and Brushton-Moira Central was no exception. It was not unusual for a new student to be bombarded with questions and treated with near celebrity status. This usually only lasted until the new kid's fate could be decided. Would the new girl be welcomed into the fold or be cast out with the other losers? Adam always thought the "new student phenomenon" would be a good psychology experiment.

He supposed Justin had chosen Michele because 1) she was new and wouldn't know about his reputation; 2) it would be easy to be the "welcoming committee" and offer to show her around town; 3) she looked like an easy conquest with her skimpy tank top and short skirt. Michele was definitely not Justin's type. She was attractive but in a vampire/metal rock kind of way. Her long, raven-black hair hung halfway down her back. She sported multiple tattoos, a nose ring, and, according to Ryan, a purple tongue ring. "There's only one reason for a girl to get her tongue pierced, right

Adam?" he asked as he repeatedly nudged Adam with his elbow. He wriggled his eyebrows up and down, and Adam pretended to know what he was talking about.

Even though Michele had a nice body and pretty gray-blue eyes, Adam was shocked to see his brother with her. He typically liked girls who were blond, big and bouncy up top, lacking self-esteem, and ditzy. Michele seemed to be the antithesis of all the qualities Justin looked for in his women. Adam wondered what he was up to then sighed in frustration because he knew exactly what his brother planned to do.

When Adam turned away from his locker, his eyes locked with Sandy's. She turned her head quickly and disappeared around the corner. She had been about twenty yards away, but Adam was sure she had been staring at him. This had been her first day back at school. She'd been absent for two days, ever since his brother had drugged her and, he could barely tolerate the thought, raped her.

Even though they only shared one study hall and lunch, Adam had been watching her. She was noticeably withdrawn. She wasn't the bubbly, sociable girl she'd once been. In the cafeteria, she had been the social butterfly, fluttering among the tables to talk with everyone. In fact, that's probably how Justin had first met her. This afternoon, Adam had watched her pick distractedly at her food, eating hardly anything at all. In study hall, she'd fallen asleep.

Adam wasn't sure what invisible force was causing him to walk in her direction, but he obeyed his legs. He walked around the corner where he'd last seen her and could see her ponytail bobbing in the distance. He watched as she exited through one of the school's side doors that led to the playing fields. He contemplated following her, but he didn't want to frighten her. *She probably thinks I'm just like him*, he thought bitterly.

*   *   *

Sandy barely made it to the exit before hot tears began to stream down her face. She hadn't wanted to go to school, but her mother had forced her, refusing to listen to her excuses of illness and cramping.

"We all get our periods, Sandy," she'd said, totally exasperated and out of patience. "You still have to go to school." She tossed a small bottle onto the foot of her bed where it landed with a soft thump. "Take some Midol and get moving. The bus will be here in twenty minutes."

Sandy hadn't told anyone what had happened. She certainly wasn't about to tell her mother. Her cheeks burned with shame whenever she thought about what Justin had done. Sandy had considered confiding in Amber, but had dismissed that idea within five seconds. She would keep this secret hidden inside herself, even though it was like a giant black hole sucking away any happiness she'd ever felt. She couldn't imagine ever being the girl she'd once been.

School had been incredibly difficult. It was a small place, and it seemed like she saw Justin around every corner. She couldn't escape him, and fear stabbed her whenever she caught a glimpse. All of her feelings were blended together to form chaos and confusion in

104

her mind. On one hand, she wanted to confront him—to yell and scream and punch. She wanted everyone to know what he was really like. On the other hand, she was scared of what he would say about her. Who would believe her? The power he held over her that night paled in comparison to the power he held over her now. Her thoughts terrified her because what she wanted most was to disappear forever, and she knew of only one way to do that.

Sandy swiped at the tears with the sleeve of her coat. There was no way she was going to get on the bus looking this way. Everyone would want to know what was wrong with her, and she was afraid of what she might say. She walked past the soccer and softball fields and followed the cross-country trail that wound through the woods. Her mother would pick her up. She would call on her cell phone and tell her she'd stayed after for extra math help. That would make her mother happy, but right now she needed to let her tears dry. She needed to construct a steel cage around her heart, and most of all, she needed time to forget.

*   *   *

Jake sat at his desk with his head in his hands. It was eight o'clock, and he could hear his grandmother watching *Wheel of Fortune* downstairs. Her voice drifted up to him, "Buy a vowel, you moron." Jake lifted his head in time to hear her berate Vanna for her "sleazy" outfit.

"Knock, knock," Papa announced as he lightly tapped on Jake's partially closed door. The door swung inward, and Jake spun around in his desk chair. His grandfather was an imposing figure at

105

six feet, four inches tall and 230 pounds. Working on the farm had kept his muscles from shriveling like most other sixty-five year olds. For a man who put the fear of God into many, Papa was a big teddy bear. He never tried to hide his emotions. Jake had seen him shed tears while burying a dead barn cat with great tenderness. He couldn't imagine how much he'd cried when his only child had been brutally murdered by her own husband. "How's your biology project coming along?" Papa stood awkwardly looking at the poster board before sitting on Jake's disheveled bed. He studied Jake's eyes carefully when he asked, "I suppose it hasn't been easy on you, has it?"

"It actually keeps getting harder. It wasn't bad at all to get information about my great-grandparents and grandparents. In fact, that turned out to be really interesting. Getting information about mom was harder, but I'm glad because I had been starting to forget her." Jake glanced up at his grandfather's sharp intake of breath.

"I don't know why we never take the time to talk about her. That was an injustice that I think we need to rectify," Papa said thoughtfully.

"I couldn't agree more," Jake said smiling. "Nana left mom's scrapbook on my bed the other night, and I couldn't stop looking at and touching everything. All these memories came flooding back. Now her face is right there when I close my eyes."

Papa leaned toward Jake and said quietly, "Actually, Jake, *I* left the scrapbook for you to look through. Your grandma still finds this difficult even after all these years. She can't stand to talk about

106

Elizabeth's death, and that's why, to some extent, we never discuss your mother with you. I realize now how wrong that was. We *need* to talk about her," Papa said emphatically, punching his open palm with his fist. Papa then noticed the red scrapbook lying on Jake's dresser. He nodded toward it. "Your grandma keeps this in the chest at the foot of our bed. I'd better put it back tonight. Whenever you want to look at it, I want you to feel free."

"Thanks, Papa, but what about Nana?" Jake didn't want Nana to think they were keeping secrets from her.

"You let me worry about her. We've been having long talks every night. I think she's starting to see things my way. She's beginning to realize that it's all right to feel sad about Elizabeth, but it's just not fair to any of us not to talk about her. I think that before long she'll show you the scrapbook herself. In the meantime, you can take it from the chest whenever you want. Just do it on the sly for right now, okay?"

"Sure." As Papa rose from Jake's bed, he hid the scrapbook under his arm. He winked at Jake as though they were conspirators in a furtive plot. "Thanks a lot, Papa, but the hardest part is still ahead." Jake pointed at the blank boxes next to his father's name.

Papa pointed at the scrapbook he still held under his arm. "Just let me return this, and I'll come back in a few minutes to help you. I did know the man for ten years. I'll know some of the information, but you'll have to call one of your other grandparents to fill in the rest."

"Thanks a lot, Papa. I couldn't bring myself to ask them when I called last week." He watched as his grandfather's broad back filled the doorway and listened as his steps echoed against the hardwood floors. Eventually, the carpet in his grandparent's bedroom swallowed the noise of his footsteps, and all was quiet once again. Jake sighed with some relief. He knew it wouldn't be easy for his grandfather to remember traits about his son-in-law, but it would be infinitely easier for Jake to have someone else struggle through this project with him.

* * *

"Dad, I need to show you something," Adam reluctantly said as he entered his father's office. This dark oak paneled room was Blake Krovlovski's sanctuary. This is where he went, Adam believed, to escape from his family. Needless to say, he spent most of his time in this room.

"Adam, I really don't have time for whatever grotesque thing your brother left to rot in your room. I have to have this brief completed and ready to show Judge Burke by seven a.m." One hand was poised over the computer's keyboard while he used a finger from the other hand to mark his place in one of the heavy law books covering his enormous desk. He hadn't bothered to look up to see the bottle of pills in Adam's hand.

Adam almost turned around and left, but he remained rooted, still six feet away from his father. He had to show him what he'd found hidden among Justin's socks. "It's not like that, dad. This is important." He took three steps to stand beside his father's leather chair and waited for him to look up. When Blake finished typing his sentence, he glanced up at his son's face. The irritation in his expression was unmistakable. Adam placed the bottle on the desk and blurted, "I found these in Justin's dresser."

Without hesitation, Blake asked, "What were you doing in his dresser?"

Adam was not surprised that his father would take his brother's side. Annoyance and anger stung him, but he continued. "Dad, do you know what these pills are? They're Rohypnol. Justin's using them to drug girls from school, so he can...you know...get what he wants out of them." Adam felt uneasy now. His father didn't appear shocked or disgusted or show any emotion whatsoever.

Blake, sounding more like a lawyer than a father, asked, "Are you certain? These are pretty wild accusations you're throwing around, Adam--accusations that could ruin a man and his reputation."

Adam couldn't help but wonder whose reputation his father was worried about...Justin's or his own? "Just look at them and then check the computer, Dad. It's Rohypnol."

Blake opened the small bottle and shook out a few pills onto his smooth palm. They were white and round and rather unassuming considering the destruction they caused. On one side were the letters ROCHE with a number one encircled beneath. On the other side, a line bisected the pill. Blake looked up at Adam and said, "Son, you did the right thing coming to me." He spun around in his chair to face the computer where Adam's accusation was confirmed with a few mouse clicks.

"I thought about going to the police..."

"I'm glad you didn't," Blake interrupted. "You would have ruined your brother's life." He stood up, dismissing Adam with a wave of his hand. "I'll take care of this right now," he said gruffly as he left his office.

Adam watched him climb the stairs to Justin's room. He was glad that his father was actually going to take charge and discipline Justin, but, on the other hand, why wasn't his father concerned about the innocent girls who'd unknowingly taken this drug?

Weren't their lives forever changed? Why was his brother's well-being more important than theirs? As a lawyer, shouldn't Blake demand justice even if his son were hurt in the process? Adam closed his eyes against the questions stampeding through his brain.

His eyes snapped open as new worries wormed their way into his mind. What would Justin do to him now that he'd told their father? Fury returned, and Adam balled his hands into fists. He didn't care what Justin did to him. He had to protect those girls from his brother. Adam thought of Sandy and unclenched his fists. He realized that nothing Justin would do to him could be worse than what he'd done to her.

*   *   *

Jake sat cross-legged on the floor while Papa lay stretched out on Jake's twin bed. His large body dwarfed the tiny bed, and his sock feet hung over the edge even though he was propped up on several

110

pillows. Jake pulled the poster board down onto the floor beside himself. He chewed on the cap of his black Expo marker and wondered where to begin. Jake knew this would be difficult for Papa, but he felt more secure with his comforting presence in the room. He glanced up at Papa and focused on his grandfather's bouncing feet. *I guess he's as nervous as I am,* Jake thought. With more confidence than he really felt, he spit the cap into his palm, placed it back onto the marker, and said, "Let's start with the easy stuff, Papa. Let's do physical characteristics. I do remember some things. I know he had brown hair and blue eyes and was tall and thin." Jake thought quietly before adding, "Just like me."

Papa sat up quickly on the bed and said gruffly, "Jake, you are not just like your dad. You may resemble him some, but you also look like your mom."

"I know," Jake whispered. "It's just really hard to think of him. I hate it. When I dream about him and Mom, I remember happy times. Then I wake up and reality slaps me in the face. It's like I can't remember Mom without remembering him."

Papa slowly got down on the floor next to Jake. "It's the same way for me, Jake, except I feel guilty. She was my daughter; I should have protected her. It's like I should have known that he was broken. I should have sensed that he would do something bad." Jake looked at his grandfather questioningly. He'd never thought about how his grandparents felt. "Were there any signs, Papa? Because if there were, I didn't see any. I don't remember arguing or yelling at all."

111

"I didn't see a thing, son. That's why I feel such remorse. I *should* have seen something. I *should* have known," he said adamantly. His eyes shone with unshed tears.

Jake laid his hand on his grandfather's knee and said, "Maybe there was nothing to see. Maybe he just flipped. That's what worries me more than anything else, Papa." Jake looked into his grandfather's eyes and felt hot tears streaming down his face. The next words were like acid on his tongue. "What if the same thing happens to me?" he choked out.

Jake felt Papa's arms engulf him. "That will *never* happen, Jake. Never."

*   *   *

Adam sat up in his bed. He wasn't sure what had awakened him, but he was wide awake. He glanced at his clock—two in the morning. He tilted his head as if to listen better. That's when he knew. He knew someone else was in the room with him. He could hear another person breathing. As his eyes adjusted to the dark, he could make out a dark shape in front of the window. He stared at it, his breaths coming in short panicked bursts. Suddenly, it came close as though gliding on air. A sharp crack sliced through the silence. Adam's cheek stung. He rolled off the other side of the bed, attempting to avoid further attack, only to knock over his bedside table. A lamp crashed to the floor. Naked fear suffocated Adam's scream; only a desperate wheezing sound escaped. He felt frozen to the floor, unable to move even though his body screamed at him to get up and run.

The figure moved closer, kneeling beside him, his breath moist and fetid against Adam's face. "You little rat." The voice seethed with anger.

"Justin?" Everything fell into place for Adam. His terror was quickly replaced with anger. "What the hell do you think you're..." His sentence ended when Justin kneeled heavily on his chest and wrapped his fingers tightly around Adam's throat. Panic flooded his body as he fought to breathe. He struggled vainly against his brother, clawing in terror at his brother's fingers. Was this lunatic the real Justin—the part he kept hidden from the outside world?

Justin leaned in close and whispered in Adam's ear. "I will fucking kill you if you ever do anything like that again. Do you understand?"

Adam was paralyzed by the venom in Justin's voice. His brother was insane, and it took only an instant for the realization to sink in—Justin *would* kill him. Of this he was certain. Adam nodded his head, ready to agree to anything as long as Justin released the vise-like grip on his throat.

Justin abruptly released his hold on Adam and shifted his weight, allowing Adam to take a shuddery breath. "You're not gonna tell Dad about this little meeting either. Got it, you little pussy?" He paused, waiting for Adam's reply. When he got none, he punched him in the ribs and sneered, "You make me sick."

Adam felt the weight lift off his chest. He took a deep breath and sat up just in time to see his bedroom door close quietly. Gingerly, he probed his neck and winced at the pain; it felt swollen and tender. His cheeks burned with tears borne of helplessness and frustration. *I guess Dad had his talk with Justin,* he thought miserably. Fighting a wave of dizziness, he stood up, turned on his bedroom light, and righted the overturned furniture. He got back into bed, keeping his bedside lamp lit and wondered what he should do.

CHAPTER 10

The next morning, Adam found himself staring into the bathroom mirror. The marks on his neck spoke of last night's violence. Ugly purple bruises, in the shape of his brother's fingers, marred his skin. He touched the skin gently, sighed, and pulled a turtleneck over his head. He also threw on a hoodie at the last minute and checked out his reflection in the mirror. Most of the bruises were now hidden. He didn't think anyone would notice the tiny bit that showed.

Adam made his way down to the kitchen. As usual, no one was there. His family never ate together, but this morning he was glad. He didn't want to see Justin or have to look his father in the eye. He felt betrayed by everyone in his family; the thought made him nauseous. He knew he wouldn't be able to stomach breakfast, so he tossed a banana and a granola bar into his backpack. Adam rushed out of the house, anxious and, he had to admit, a bit afraid of running into his brother. He just couldn't forget the depravity in Justin's voice last night. It's not as if he'd ever had a great relationship with his brother, but last night Justin was a stranger. Adam had never before encountered that level of malevolence.

*   *   *

Jake helped himself to another of the chocolate chip pancakes Nana had made for breakfast. "Thanks, Nana, these really hit the spot." Jake had finished his morning chores, taken a shower and hustled down the stairs when the scent of pancakes reached him in his bedroom.

"You're welcome, sweetie. Your mom always loved these pancakes. They were her favorite." She sighed wistfully, pulled out a chair to sit across from Jake and continued. "I always made them when she was feeling blue."

Jake almost stopped eating. He was so surprised to hear Nana talking about his mom. He didn't want to break the spell, though, so he continued eating slowly, only now he was savoring each word that passed over his grandmother's lips.

"She was so passionate about animals when she was younger that I always thought she'd become a veterinarian. Once, when she was about seven or eight, she saved a litter of kittens. Your Papa was pretty sure that the mother cat was killed by the German shepherd that lived down the road. He'd seen that dog carrying some poor dead creature in its jaws earlier that morning. Of course, he didn't tell Elizabeth about what he'd seen. She would have cried for sure. I don't remember what tale he invented, but I'm sure it was a good one involving some cat prince or something. She was always a sucker for the 'happily ever after.'" Nana stirred her coffee and looked distracted. She had suddenly realized that her daughter, the one who believed in happy endings, had never had one for herself.

Jake could tell his grandmother was suffering. He knew he had to bring her back to the present. "Nana, what happened to the kittens? How did she save them?"

Nana looked at Jake as though surprised to see him sitting across from her. "Oh," she said visibly bringing herself back to her story. She sat upright, a smile beginning to curl at her lips. "Well,

116

my Elizabeth brought those babies right into her room. She fed them with one of her baby doll's bottles and set up a cozy little bed right beside her own. Now, Jake...these babies were only a week old at most, so your mama had to rub their bellies to make them pee and poop. Your grandfather showed her how to do it, and all those babies lived because of her." Nana smiled at the memory.

"What happened to the kittens? Did you keep them all?" Jake asked curiously.

"They stayed in Elizabeth's room for a while until I realized they were healthy enough to go to the barn. She had been telling me that they were too weak to return, but one night I caught the little buggers."

"What were they doing?" Jake asked with interest, his breakfast long forgotten.

"Your mom was already asleep and I was just checking in on her. Those little kitties, who were supposed to be sleeping in the box next to her bed, were using the blanket to climb into bed with her." Nana laughed out loud. "I watched for a few minutes until all five of those kittens were snuggled up with Elizabeth. Even though it was cute, I didn't want five housecats, so Elizabeth made a cat hotel in the barn for them using all sorts of boxes she found. Those were the most spoiled cats in creation."

Jake smiled at Nana who grinned back at him. "Thanks for telling me that story. Do you know why she didn't become a vet?"

"Yes, she changed her mind in high school. She said she just couldn't bear to see any animals in pain. She loved them too much."

"That makes sense. By then she would have seen a lot of the suffering that goes on at the farm. It makes me depressed too to see an animal in pain."

"I know, honey. You're sensitive like your mom. She would be very proud of you." Nana stood and collected Jake's dirty dishes. "You'd better get yourself to school, young man. I might have just made you late with my recollections."

Jake looked quickly at the clock and back to his grandma. "It's okay; it was worth every second." He kissed her on the top of the head, slung his backpack over his shoulder, and headed out the door.

When Jake pulled into Amber's driveway, he saw her waiting on her porch steps. She stood, looked at an imaginary watch, and tapped her foot impatiently. She tried to appear angry but looked more like a cartoon character. She began laughing as Jake leapt from the truck and jogged the few steps to her. He lifted her off her feet in a huge bear hug and spun her around.

"What's that all about," Amber giggled as Jake set her down. "I guess that's one way to apologize for making me wait four and a half minutes."

"You were right," Jake blurted excitedly.

"I'm always right, Jake. You have to be more specific."

"Nana told me a story about my mom when she was young. She told me all on her own without me asking her or anything." Jake ushered her into the truck.

"Wow, I guess your grandpa has been talking to her. He's a pretty persuasive guy, isn't he?"

Jake climbed in beside her. "I think this is all going to work out. We can stop walking on eggshells around each other and finally talk about mom. I guess this project has been good for something." Jake looked sideways at Amber and added, "Although I'll never tell Mrs. Drake that."

When they pulled into the parking lot at school, Jake felt happier than he had in a while. A weight had been lifted from his shoulders.

*   *   *

"Dude, why don't you just grow a pair and ask her out?" Ryan asked Adam during lunch.

"What?" Adam asked, confused.

"Sandy. You've been staring at her for the past ten minutes. Just ask her out and quit staring like some mental patient. You're going to freak her out if you keep acting like a stalker." He opened his carton of chocolate milk and took three huge swallows that completely emptied it. "I won't even stand in your way. She's too young for me," he added good-naturedly.

Adam looked at Ryan and shook his head in disbelief. "I don't want to ask her out. I was just noticing…"

"What—her boobs?" Ryan interrupted. "They are pretty nice for a freshman, aren't they?" Ryan was now the one staring at Sandy.

"You are such an ass sometimes. What I was trying to say is that I've noticed that she's acting differently. She seems quieter and unhappy." Adam noticed Ryan's blank look. "Don't you pay attention to anything that doesn't look back at you in the mirror? Look...she's sitting all by herself. Have you ever seen her by herself? Usually, she's surrounded by friends or gossiping with Amber."

"Geez, I'm so sorry, Mr. Observant. I guess I won't be getting that detective badge anytime soon." Ryan's words virtually with sarcasm. "Why do you care so much anyway? Have you ever even had a conversation with her before that lasted more than two minutes?" Ryan shoved half of his hot dog in his mouth before continuing. Adam had to look away to avoid the sight of half-chewed food. "Don't get me wrong...I can see why you've been watching her. She's smokin' hot, but why are you playing therapist all the sudden? You're usually the first one to point out a nice rack."

"Never mind," Adam mumbled. "Unlike you, I have the ability to feel sympathy for another person." Adam abruptly picked up his lunch tray and briskly walked to the garbage can where he dumped his mostly uneaten lunch. He felt stupid for trying to talk to Ryan. He should have known that he would just say something stupid.

Ryan watched his friend leave the cafeteria and wondered what he'd done wrong. He looked over at Sandy and studied her carefully. She did look different, now that he'd bothered to look. Her clothes looked rumpled, as though she'd slept in them and her hair, which usually looked like it had taken hours to do, was simply pulled back into a messy ponytail.

"Hey, Ryan, where's Adam?" Jake asked as he sat down. He began eating before Ryan could respond.

"You just missed him. He got pissed at me because apparently I'm a self-centered douche."

"Tell me something I don't know," Jake responded as he slapped Ryan good-naturedly on the back.

"Where have you been, anyway? You might have saved me from Adam's guilt trip," Ryan asked as he pushed away his lunch tray.

"Amber and I were with Mrs. Sevey working on our English project. Amber's still there. We have to write *and* perform a slam poem as one of the characters from *To Kill a Mockingbird*."

"Sounds real fun," Ryan mumbled as he stared across the room.

Jake followed his line of sight and realized Ryan was looking at Sandy. He turned toward Ryan and was surprised to see him looking pensively, not lustfully, at the beautiful girl. "Why the long face? Did she turn you down, or what," Jake asked jokingly.

Ryan faced Jake. "See...you didn't notice either. You're just as much an asshole as I am."

"Whoa, whoa! Slow down!" Jake raised his hands in surrender. "I can't compare with you in the asshole department and you know that. You're the reigning champ and I will never deny you of your title." Ryan didn't even smirk at his comment, and Jake wondered if he'd gone too far. He began to wonder if maybe Ryan was actually upset about something. "All right...tell me what happened with Adam and what your little spat has to do with Sandy."

"It's really not that big a deal, but you know how Adam gets. He's like super-sensitive about other people, and he noticed that Sandy has been looking unhappy. Then he got mad at me when I didn't notice. I mean, what am I, a shrink? I don't pay attention to other people's moods."

"We all know that. Adam certainly should be used to you by now." Things didn't add up for Jake, and he wasn't entirely sure if Ryan was telling him the entire story. "He left the cafeteria because of *that*? Are you sure there's not more?"

"Well, I did make a crack about her boobs, but he mostly got angry because I didn't notice that she was acting all depressed."

"Dude, you can't go three minutes without talking about someone's boobs. I've even seen you checking out mine."

Ryan reached out playfully and grabbed one of Jake's pectoral muscles. "They are pretty sweet."

Jake swatted away his hand and laughed. "What I'm trying to say, without getting molested, is that maybe something else is on Adam's mind. It probably has to do with his family. You know how they get along…like oil and water, as Nana would say."

                    *   *   *

Hi, Mrs. Krovlovski, is Adam here?" Ryan asked. Adam's stepmother was wearing a bikini and drinking a margarita while standing at the sink. Ryan couldn't help but notice that Pasquel was directly outside the window cutting back the rose bushes.

"How many times have I told you, Ryan, to call me Julia?" She smiled sweetly. "Would you like a soda--or maybe a beer?" She made her way to the refrigerator and leaned inside, offering Ryan a good look and not just at the contents of the fridge.

"Um…no thanks. I was just looking for Adam." For all of Ryan's swagger, Mrs. Krovlovski made him feel extremely awkward. He shifted uncomfortably and looked around as though Adam might walk in at any moment.

"He's in his room. Go on up." She gestured casually toward the stairs, dismissing Ryan, and returned back to the window where Pasquel was now shirtless. She needed a man, not a boy, but she would never tire of making Ryan squirm.

Ryan knocked sharply on Adam's closed door, but there was no response. "Adam, are you in there?" he called out.

The door opened quickly as though Adam had been standing right there. "Oh, it's you," Adam said relieved.

"Were you expecting someone else?" he asked teasingly as he entered the room. Ryan flopped on the leather recliner, leaned back, and made himself at home.

"What are you doing here?" Adam asked, distracted.

"Can't a guy just drop in on his friend?" Ryan sat back up in the chair and looked closely at Adam. He was wearing an old tattered t-shirt, and the bruises were now evident on his neck. "What the hell happened to you?" he asked rising quickly from the chair and pointing at Adam's throat.

Adam attempted to shield Ryan's view, but he'd already seen the damage. "It's nothing. Justin and I were wrestling last night, and he got a little overexcited."

"Are those finger marks? That's not wrestling, Adam, that's an attempt to wring your friggin' neck. Did you tell your dad?"

Adam sat heavily on his bed. "No, I can't tell him."

"Why not?"

Adam lay back on his bed and pulled his pillow over his face. He knew this problem was much larger than himself, and he needed someone's advice. He was even desperate enough to take some from Ryan. They'd been friends since sixth grade when Adam had moved to the area and, even though Ryan was a pain in the ass most of the time, he knew he could count on him when he needed serious help. At the very least, Ryan was pretty inventive, so maybe he could figure out a plan. He yanked the pillow from his face and sat up. "What I'm about to tell you is some serious shit. I'm only telling you because I don't know what to do." He watched Ryan's face drain of color. "Before I say anything, do you think you can help me without making everything a million times worse?"

Ryan was worried. He'd never seen Adam so upset, not even when he'd caught Pasquel banging Julia in the tool shed. He looked Adam in the eye and solemnly said, "You can trust me. I'll do whatever I can to help."

Once Adam began, he could not stop. His words rushed forth like a waterfall, unstoppable and full of fury. He told Ryan about his brothers' "competition," about seeing Sandy fleeing the house, about finding Rohypnol in his brother's drawer, and finally about his brother's death threat the night before. "I don't know what to do. He's crazy. Dad will probably disown me if I go to the police."

124

Adam's face crumbled; an onslaught of tears rained down his cheeks.

Ryan sat down next to him on the bed and clasped his shoulder. "Jesus, you *are* stuck between a rock and a hard place aren't you? What a twisted bunch of freaks live here," he said shaking his head in dismay. "It's a wonder you're not a total fuckup."

"What do I do?" Adam pleaded.

"Well, first things first. You're going to pack up some stuff and come home with me. That'll stop the middle of the night stealth attacks. We'll figure out the other stuff later. Man, that dipshit had better be glad he's not home right now." Ryan punched his hand menacingly. "I'd kick his ass so hard he wouldn't remember his name." A door slammed from somewhere down the hall. Ryan looked around anxiously. "He's *not* home, right?"

"No, killer. He's still at football practice." Adam wiped at the tears and smiled at Ryan's obvious relief.

"All right, then…stop crying and get your shit together. I've got to get out of this loony bin."

Adam knew it wouldn't be a problem staying at Ryan's house. He could probably stay away for three to four days before anyone would even realize he was gone. He haphazardly tossed some clothes into a duffel bag. The two boys left the house, Adam feeling better for having confided in Ryan. He now had someone else to share his burden.

*　　*　　*

"Hey, Grandpa, it's me, Jake." He held the phone receiver in one hand as he tried to jam a bunch of carefully matched socks into his top drawer. He fought to close it; Nana hated to see clothes hanging out of half-opened drawers.

"Hi there, Jakey. How's your running going?"

"It's going really well. I've been gunning for Franklin Academy's top runner, and I've been closing the gap. I got real close to him last week, so I think I'll be able to catch him when we race at the state meet in a couple of weeks." After dropping in a sweatshirt, Jake closed the bottom drawer of his dresser with his foot and sat at his desk. He purposely turned away from where his biology notebook glared at him. He wanted to have a normal conversation with his grandfather before he'd have to broach the subject of his father.

"I read about that race. I check the newspaper archives on the Internet once a week just to keep track of you, you know. He only got you by six seconds. You'll get him next time," Grandpa Carver stated with confidence.

"Jeez, you're getting more computer savvy than I am. I didn't realize that *The Telegram* even posted on the Internet. They're really moving up in the world, aren't they," Jake joked.

"I guess everyone needs to keep up with the changing times. Even your grandmother wants to buy one of those I-Pads, but I think she should find a cheaper way to pass her time," he said with a chuckle as his wife looked past her romance novel to give him 'the look' she'd spent the last forty years perfecting. As he walked into the kitchen, he added wistfully, "I wish you didn't live four hours away. Spoiling her grandson would keep her busy, and we'd be able to watch all of your races. It's too bad that we can only see one or two each season. Will you race in Vermont again this year?"

"No, but I was glad you got to go to the race in Essex last month."

"That was a pretty simple decision. You were only an hour away from us then, and we had a really good time."

Jake cleared his throat and spun back around to face his desk. There was no point in prolonging the inevitable. "Grandpa, I called because I have to ask a few more questions for my biology project. Only this time," Jake paused, "I have to ask about my father." There was a moment of awkward silence before Jake heard his grandfather's footsteps and a door open and close.

"I figured you'd be asking about Greg at some point. Whoever heard about doing a genetics project without taking the father into account?" Mr. Carver blew out a gust of air as he walked across the front porch to settle into a rocking chair. He didn't want his wife to overhear the conversation. She always became extremely anxious whenever Greg was mentioned. "Okay, I'm ready…ask away."

"Well, could you tell me a bit about his time in school? What kind of student was he? Did he get good grades? Was he involved in sports? That sort of thing." Jake sped through the questions, hoping to end the uncomfortable discussion.

Mr. Carver watched, captivated, as three of the neighborhood boys raced by on their bikes. Their jubilant shouts became lost as they sped down the sidewalk. He preferred to remember easier times, when his own children were young and full of life. The weight of the phone brought him back to the present. "Greg," he started, his voice cracking on the name, "certainly wasn't a student like you are." He rarely spoke of his son and had to clear away the cobwebs in his throat. "He didn't have your motivation or drive, and he hated to read. He claimed it gave him headaches."

Mr. Carver gave an uneasy laugh and shifted in his seat. "His English teachers used to call us all the time to complain about his work ethic. He was a real whiz at math and science, though, and he liked to take apart everything just to see if he could put it together again. Lucky for him, he was good at that. I'll never forget the look on your grandma's face when she came home to find her new dishwasher spread across the kitchen floor. Pieces were everywhere. I thought she'd have a coronary right then and there. I had to take her out to dinner, and by the time we got back, that machine was right as rain once again. He was always curious as to how things worked."

Jake wasn't sure how to react to this information. Did he want to resemble his father at all? He *loved* to read and especially liked mystery books, but he also liked math and science and, just the other day, helped Papa fix the motor on the old tractor. Were someone's interests genetically inherited? He was almost afraid to ask the next question. "Did he play any school sports?"

"Nope, he had no interest at all in organized sports."

Jake was relieved at this dissimilarity. He loved all sports.

128

"But he was a heck of a natural athlete," Mr. Carver continued. "He played all kinds of sports with his buddies. He just didn't play school sports because he was too busy tinkering around with his tools." It was easier now; his voice was stronger. It was much better to remember him as a child instead of the man he'd become.

"Oh," Jake replied glumly. He was actually a lot like his father. "Papa helped me with some of the physical characteristics, but he couldn't remember his exact height. How tall was he?" Jake asked, already knowing that they were close in height.

"Let's see…he's six feet, three inches. He was never built like you, though. You're what I'd call wiry, tall and thin with a small frame, but your father had a lot of muscle mass and broad shoulders."

A silence followed as both realized what Greg's muscles had done to Jake's mother.

Mr. Carver felt a weight on his chest. He had to speak…to say the things he'd never before said to his grandson. He cleared his throat nervously. "This is the first time we've ever talked about your father, and that's fine. He did an unspeakable thing. We loved Elizabeth like she was our own daughter. We've never forgiven him either, but it's also hard for us to forget all the good memories your grandmother and I have of him. His actions were shocking to us as well. We never saw anything like that coming."

A lump formed in Jake's throat, and tears threatened to spill down his cheeks.

His grandfather's voice broke. "You see him as a monster, and I will never say you're wrong, but I know, with absolute certainty, that he loved you and your mother. I would give anything to know why he did what he did. It breaks our hearts to wonder if we did something wrong while raising him."

Jake knew his grandfather was crying and wished he could give him comfort, but words would be a useless bandage when the truth could be the only salve that would heal. When he eventually hung up with his grandfather, he pondered the guilt his grandparents had heaped upon themselves.

*   *   *

"Hey, Dad, it's me." There was silence at the other end of the phone line. Adam rolled his eyes. "It's Adam," he said, barely containing the anger from his voice. "I'm staying at Ryan's for a few nights. I just wanted you to know where I was so you wouldn't worry." Adam knew his father wouldn't have wasted more than five minutes worrying about his youngest son's whereabouts, but he thought he'd throw that in just to see how his father would react.

"Okay…that's fine," Blake answered distractedly. "I'm still at the office trying to keep ahead of some paperwork."

Ryan and Adam had formed a semblance of a game plan earlier that evening. "We need to know if your dad is actually taking this Justin thing seriously. If he's not, we'll have to go to a higher power. He can't go unpunished. You know that, don't you?" Ryan had asked earlier.

Adam was deeply relieved to hear those words from Ryan. That's exactly what he wanted to do. He'd just needed to hear the advice from a third party. He knew he had to do the right thing. And just maybe, his father was actually doing something about the situation. "Dad, what exactly are you going to do about Justin?"

"What do you mean what am I going to do with him? I told him to stop doing what he was doing." Anger crept into Blake's voice.

"That's it? You told him to stop? Do you really think that's going to cut it?" Adam was no longer nervous; he was furious.

"I flushed the pills down the toilet, I took away his car, and…what am I doing here? I don't have to explain myself to you! I've taken care of the situation and that's the end of it. I'm extremely busy here, so…"

"Of course, you're busy. You're always too busy!" Adam shouted into the phone before hanging up. He walked out of the bathroom where he'd gone for privacy. He was emotionally drained. "I don't know why I expected something more from him," he mumbled as he walked toward Ryan's bedroom.

"Don't keep me in suspense, Adam. What did he say?" Ryan asked.

Adam quickly summarized the conversation. "As far as I'm concerned, my father is just as bad as Justin."

"What would have been a satisfying answer, Adam?" Ryan asked curiously.

"I don't know," Adam replied glumly as he cleared some dirty clothes from a chair. "I guess I wanted him to sound angry and disappointed with Justin, but he just sounds mad at me. What did I do? I'm trying to help and do what's right. I guess a part of me wanted dad to get Justin into therapy or something. That would have been a start to finding a solution. Instead, he just finds excuses. He just doesn't want his reputation ruined. That's all he cares about." Adam glanced over at Ryan. He was a little surprised at how serious and helpful Ryan was being. He really was a decent guy…he just kept it hidden. "So, now what do we do?"

"Well, since your dad is about as useless as a gay guy in a whorehouse, I guess this means we carry on with Plan B," Ryan said with a smirk. "Get your game-face on. This is going to take some planning."

*　　*　　*

"I'm sorry, Amber, but I have to watch my cousins this weekend." Sandy wished she'd never answered the phone. She hated lying to her friend, but the thought of spending time alone with anyone made her extremely anxious. She knew that she would tell Amber what Justin had done to her. She would spill her guts in no time flat, and that's exactly what she had to avoid at all costs.

"Are you sure you can't get out of it? It's supposed to be a really good movie, but since it's a total chick-flick, Jake's not going to want to see it." Actually, Amber knew that Jake would make the ultimate sacrifice and sit through a romantic movie with her, but she was trying to figure out how to spend some time with Sandy. She was definitely not acting like herself lately. "We haven't hung out in a long time," she wheedled.

Sandy tried to make her voice light. "Sorry, but I can't back out now. She asked me last week." In an attempt to end the conversation she added, "I'll see you at school tomorrow."

"Wait...don't hang up," Amber blurted. "Are you sure you're okay? You missed Monday and Tuesday, you're acting like a zombie at school, and if I had low self-esteem, I'd think you were trying to blow me off. You're avoiding everyone like the plague. Do you want to talk about anything?" she asked.

"There's nothing wrong, Amber. Really. I missed school because I was wicked sick. You don't want to know about the stuff that came out of me. Trust me; it would make you gag." It wasn't difficult to lie; she really did feel sick. "I probably should've missed Wednesday and today too, but I can't miss *four* days of school. I would never be able to catch up. It's hard enough missing just two days. I'm not that smart; you know that first hand." Sandy made a half-hearted attempt at a giggle. She wanted nothing more than to end this conversation, but she didn't want to arouse Amber's suspicion any more.

Amber laughed too, remembering the day Sandy confused Sigmund Freud with Siegfried and Roy. That's part of the reason why she liked Sandy so much. Like Adam, she oftentimes said unintentionally funny things that had everyone rolling with laughter, but she never got mad. She was self-deprecating but self-assured at the same time. "Do you think you should be babysitting your cousins if you're that sick? What if it's catchy?" Amber asked. She wasn't convinced one hundred percent, but Sandy had never lied to her before.

Shit, Sandy thought. *She has me there.* "Hold on a sec, Amber. My mom's yelling something."

Amber patted the bed beside her, and Spencer jumped. It took him two tries before he made it, but he settled in beside her and rolled onto his back to have his belly rubbed. Amber could hear Sandy's muffled voice as she shouted downstairs to her mother.

"Dinner's ready," Sandy explained. "I'm going to try solid food tonight since everything stayed down today. I'll see you tomorrow," she said before hanging up.

Amber stared at the phone before tossing it on the bed beside Spencer. The call had ended a bit abruptly, but maybe Sandy was finally getting back her appetite. Amber grabbed the novel for English class off her bedside table and vowed to track down Sandy the next day at school.

Sandy looked at the silent phone she still held in her hand. Could she tell her, she wondered. She thought about calling Amber back, but, instead, replaced the phone to its cradle. She walked downstairs...alone. She would sit at the kitchen table and pick at some leftovers...alone. She would suffer through the barbs of shame, the arrows of regret, and the lashes of anger...alone.

*   *   *

Jake stared thoughtfully at his completed biology project. The poster board, now rolled up tightly and secured with three rubber bands, lay across his three-page family genetics essay. Relief made him euphoric; he was glad to be done, but, at the same time, he was thankful for all he had discovered. It hadn't been easy, but Mrs. Drake had been right when she'd told him he was stronger than he thought.

He almost felt guilty when he reflected on Mrs. Drake's lessons on nature versus nurture. Here he was so worried that he'd inherited his father's bad genes while his grandparents worried that they'd somehow raised a broken son. His father had two other siblings: Aunt Lisa and Uncle George. His aunt was a third grade teacher and had two of her own kids, and Uncle George worked in a bank doing something or other with loans. He was married as well, but they had no children. They had normal lives, so obviously his grandparents weren't bad parents. What had made his father do the unthinkable?

Jake crawled into bed and pulled the covers up to his chin. He was suddenly chilled. He longed to put all this behind him, but, as he tossed and turned, an endless litany of questions and possibilities assailed his thoughts. He finally fell into a deep slumber at two am.

Jake's sleep was cut short when he sat up with a start. He looked at his clock. It was 4:30 in the morning. *He's six feet, three inches. He was never built like you, though. You're what I'd call wiry, tall and thin with a small frame, but your father had a lot of muscle mass and broad shoulders.* His grandfather's words echoed in his ears, but one phrase repeated over and over in his mind. *He's six feet, three inches.* Jake tossed and turned fitfully. Sleep evaded him. *He's six feet, three inches.*

CHAPTER 11

He could feel the dark time approaching, but he could not stop it any more than he could stop an avalanche. The voices around him slowly became an indecipherable hum. His own fork remained suspended midway to his mouth, fixed in place, and he watched, mesmerized, while everything around him slowed. Everyone moved as though underwater before finally coming to a dead standstill. Time had stopped, waiting patiently for what would come next. The edges of the man's vision blurred before he saw everything again with sudden clarity.

He heard it. One sound emerging from the silence and rising louder and louder, a knife stabbing his brain. He dropped his fork, covered his ears, and zeroed in on it—a clinking noise that grew louder and more intense with each passing second. He saw him then. The tattooed man sat halfway down the table eating his stew with relish, his spoon scraping the side of the bowl. No one moved, except for this man. Everyone else was frozen in place, captured, mid-sentence, mid-step, as though unwilling participants in some crazy photo shoot. Rage consumed his entire body, his nerve endings fired rapidly, and his whole body became rigid with suppressed action.

He walked swiftly and surely over to the man, who barely had time to see the metal tray swinging toward his face. Blood splattered across the other diners, who sat unflinchingly. He couldn't stop himself. Something commanded him now—a primal urge he'd known before. Brain matter oozed through the smashed skull but still he swung the tray, frenzied and out of control. The wet thumping sound created a nauseating rhythm, but its familiarity comforted him—he'd known it before. When he finally stopped, the tattooed man was dead, a pool of blood growing around his head, a halo of gore that he'd known before. Greg Carver stood over him, exhausted yet content. He could taste metal, almost as though he had a mouthful of pennies, but he knew it was blood.

Greg squeezed his eyes closed tightly. A layer of quiet wrapped itself around him, reassuring him. But, there it was. Slowly it returned…the clinking noise. The sound grew in intensity until Greg's eyelids flew open. The tattooed man was there, eating his stew. How could that be?

"Are you deaf, asshole? I said your lip is bleeding, and I don't need none of your diseases."

Greg turned, dazed, to the man beside him. "What?" he asked.

The man mumbled disgustedly as he stood and left.

Greg could taste the blood in his mouth and realized that he'd bitten through his bottom lip.

CHAPTER 12

"Cat got your tongue?" Amber asked, nudging Jake's arm playfully with her elbow. They'd driven the five minutes from her house to school, and the only thing Jake had said was a half hearted, "Hi."

He maneuvered the truck into his usual spot near the rusty dumpsters at the farthest corner of the school parking lot. "Sorry. I didn't get a lot of sleep." Jake shook his head as though to clear away a fog. "I talked with Grandpa Carver last night."

"That's great," Amber said cheerily. When Jake didn't respond she added, "Isn't it? That means your project's all done, right?"

"Yes, it's all done," Jake sighed dramatically. "Finally."

"Then why are you acting like someone flushed your pet fish? You should be happy." The two exited the truck and walked slowly toward the school's entrance. Amber knew something was still bothering Jake. She took his hand and moved in front of him so he could no longer avoid her eyes. A steady stream of students just getting off the buses flowed around them. "So…what's wrong? Did you find out something else?" she prompted.

Jake turned away from Amber's penetrating gaze and guided her away from the busy entrance and over to the empty playground. "You know how I've been worried about sharing my father's bad genes?"

Amber nodded. She had found that, with Jake, her silence almost always prompted him to talk.

"Well, I just found out that my grandparents blame themselves for what happened." He kicked at a stone and watched it tumble against the curb. It was difficult to explain the uneasy feeling that had settled into his gut. "I guess it just upsets me because I've never thought about how they felt, and now that I'm older, I feel sort of selfish for not thinking about their feelings."

Jake's sensitivity amazed Amber. Here he was thinking the worst about himself when he actually spent more time than any other teenager thinking about how other people felt. "Jake, you've got to stop beating yourself up," she implored. She grasped his shoulders and gently turned him so he couldn't avoid her eyes. "The only reason you've never thought about it is because you've hidden this whole part of your life. You haven't *thought* about it at all. All this does is prove that you're a caring person who's always thinking of others." She smiled at him. "It makes me a little sick, actually," she added lightly. She led him to the swings. "Get on," she motioned, "I'll push. A little swing in the morning will make anyone feel better."

Jake looked dubious but sat on the swing anyway. Amber began pushing him gently. "There is one more thing," Jake said slowly, wondering how these words would sound to someone else's ears. "My grandfather said something...something that I just can't get out of my mind. It's all I can think about. I mean, these words woke me up out of a deep sleep," he added to convey their importance.

The swing screeched impatiently, as though it, too, waited for Jake to continue. Amber stopped pushing him, but Jake still swayed forward and backward. "What did he say?" Amber asked quietly when Jake remained silent.

"He said my father is six feet, three inches tall."

Amber stepped in front of the now silent swing. "That's not unusual. You're just about that tall, aren't you?"

"Don't you get it?" Jake asked irritably. "He said he *is*...he *is*."

"Oh," she replied, finally realizing why those words would haunt him. She waved her hand casually. "I'm sure that was just a slip of the tongue. You said your father cut his..." Amber couldn't bring herself to continue. Just thinking of a person slitting his own throat made her shiver. "He killed himself," she amended. "Your grandfather probably isn't used to talking about your father either, so he reverted back to the present tense. I'm sure it was just a mistake," she continued reassuringly.

The warning bell blasted over the loudspeaker, indicating they now had three minutes to be in their respective homerooms. She held out her hands to him and pulled him out of the swing.

As Jake stood, he wrapped an arm around Amber's waist and guided her toward the school. "I'm sure you're right, and I keep telling myself the same thing, but..." His tongue fumbled for the right words. "It was just really weird to wake suddenly with my grandfather's voice saying those words over and over again. I'm sure you're right," he repeated, in an attempt to convince himself. "It was just a mistake." The two merged with the other students streaming into the building. "I'll see you in English." Jake leaned in and gave Amber a quick kiss on the lips.

She, in turn, swatted him on the butt as he turned toward math class. "Peace out, cub scout."

Jake couldn't help but smile. Telling Amber *had* made him feel better. His mood brightened some, but his grandfather's words sat waiting at the edge of his brain.

*   *   *

The first part of Plan B was Sandy. Ryan thought it would be best if Adam could convince her to go to the police or even to a teacher or school counselor. That way, Adam wouldn't be forever branded as the family narc. "This way is just better, Adam," he'd explained. "If you go the cops, they're going to have to interview Sandy anyway. Either way, she'll have to tell them what happened. Maybe she'll be more likely to report it if she knows that you can back up her story."

The plan made perfect sense when Ryan had explained it to him, but how was he going to confront Sandy? It had been about a week since the rape, and he hadn't said a thing to her. How would she react when he said he wanted to help now? She was sure to hate him. How would he even get her alone with him? The good feelings he'd had that morning were quickly vanishing. His stomach somersaulted as he watched Sandy slink into room B-4 where they both had study hall.

Her transformation was unbelievable. She no longer wore her contact lenses, wearing, instead, a pair of thick, black-framed glasses. Her once tight clothes were replaced by a baggy T-shirt (which probably belonged to her father and hung past her butt) and a pair of baggy cargo pants. Some dingy Converse sneakers completed her new androgynous look. How could everyone be so blind? She was advertising her suffering on a giant billboard, but no one seemed to care. Adam entered the room as the bell rang.

"Here's the library pass. Who wants to go?" Mr. Compeau waved the pink sheet in the air, distracted by his crossword puzzle. He slapped the pass on a nearby desk and mumbled, "Make sure the last person takes the pass. I don't need the librarian on my butt again. The rest of you…find something to do." He waved his hand absently at the students as though he didn't really care what they did as long as they didn't interrupt his puzzle solving time.

Adam noticed Sandy signing the library pass. He stood up as soon as she left, joined the other two students at the desk, and added his name to the pass as well. He took his time walking down the stairs; he didn't want Sandy to think that he was following her. She had managed to avoid their study hall fairly well by going to other teachers' classrooms, presumably to make up the classes she had missed after the "incident." He walked through the double glass doors and met an icy wall. The library was one of the few rooms that had air conditioning, and he wondered, once again, why the school always had the A/C blasting when it was cold outside and never in May or June when everyone was roasting to death.

He saw Sandy sitting at a corner table, as far from anyone as she could possibly get. There were about ten students in the computer lab, a few others scattered at tables, and one girl sitting cross-legged on the floor browsing through the bookshelves. Adam set his books down at a table near Sandy and sat so he could make eye contact. She looked up when his books thudded heavily and quickly averted her eyes. Did he see fear, shame, disappointment, anger or a combination? He couldn't be sure. Sandy stood, grabbed randomly at one of the reference books on the shelf nearby, and returned to her table. Only now, she sat in a different chair so that her back was facing him. So much for making eye contact.

Adam spent the rest of the period pretending to do his homework, but his mind was reeling. How was he going to get Sandy to talk to him when she couldn't even face him from ten feet away? *This just isn't going to work*, he thought miserably. With only five minutes left of the period, Adam scrawled a note. He rose to speak to the librarian and, on the way, dropped the folded paper on Sandy's table just seconds before the bell rang.

*   *   *

Sandy closed the bathroom's stall door behind her, locked it, and sat heavily on the toilet seat. A mob of girls entered and gathered around the mirror. Sandy watched through the gap beside the door as they applied additional makeup, checked their hair, and dished out the latest gossip. She listened to their chatter and wished she could once again be like those foolish girls who hadn't a worry in the world. She waited until the late bell rang and for everyone else to leave before she took the folded up note from her purse. She held it in her sweaty hands and stared at it, wondering if she should even read its message.

She didn't really know Adam that well. He'd been at the gorge all summer, and he was in her study hall this year, but it's not like they'd ever had a meaningful conversation. What she did know about him made her stomach turn--he was Justin's brother, and if they were brothers, they were probably just alike. She balled up the note, intent on throwing it into the metal garbage receptacle screwed onto the wall beside the toilet, but she hesitated. Adam didn't seem like Justin; he was definitely not a player. All the girls thought he was a goofball, but he still followed them around like a puppy. He'd be lucky to get a date to the Prom. Maybe he wasn't like his brother at all. Justin had never even mentioned Adam, but he'd talked her ear off about his older brother, Charles.

She turned the paper over and over in her hands. What would it say? She took a deep breath and unfolded the paper. There was only one way to find out.

Sandy,

I know what Justin did to you that night. I saw you leave the house and got suspicious. I found the drug he gave you. I didn't know that was his plan. You have to believe me. I want to help you. I think we need to talk to someone about what happened so it doesn't happen to someone else. I think he's done it before. I wish I could have helped that night, but I want to help now. I'm really sorry. I'll find you in lunch so we can talk.--Adam

Tears rolled across Sandy's cheeks and fell, unchecked, onto Adam's note. So he *had* been there. He knew the truth. A swarm of emotions relentlessly stung her as she sat in stunned silence. She felt embarrassment that Adam knew what happened, anger that he did nothing to rescue her, wariness at his offer to help, and shame at her own stupidity. Could she trust Adam?

Sandy hurriedly pulled at the roll of toilet paper and swiped at her eyes. She crumpled the tear-stained letter and shoved it back into her purse. Did she want his help? If they told one of the counselors at school, they'd call her parents and probably force her to go to the police. Then everyone would know. Did she want that? Definitely not. She could already hear the rumors spreading like wildfire across the entire town. She knew deep-down that none of this was her fault, but she just couldn't face the attention and sympathetic stares once everyone found out. And besides, Justin's father was a lawyer. She'd watched enough cop shows to know that lawyers made the victims look like total sluts.

Sandy weighed her options. Adam made it sound like she wasn't the only one who'd been enticed by Justin's web of deception. What happened if he did it to another unsuspecting freshman? Would she feel badly? She knew she would, but she also didn't want to feel like that Hester Prynne lady they'd read about in English. What letter would the court pin to her chest...an "I" for Idiot...a "G" for Gullible? Who would want to be forever branded as the moron who fell for Justin Krovlovski's tricks?

When she finally left the stall's sanctuary, she was startled by her reflection in the mirror. Her eyes were red and puffy, her hair was a mess, and she was deathly pale, but she didn't care about her appearance anymore. In fact, she didn't care about much of anything and that included being late to science lab. She pulled open the bathroom door with more force than necessary. It banged against the wall, an explosion in the otherwise quiet hallway. She strode toward her classroom with more composure than she actually felt and ignored the hall monitor who called out to her disapprovingly. Her footsteps fell hollowly on the shiny, black tiled floor.

*   *   *

Sandy couldn't concentrate during any of her classes. Lunch was approaching, and her mind was busy wrestling with the decision only she could make. When the bell rang, Sandy made her way through the maze of cafeteria tables and chairs. She rehearsed what she would say to Adam. She sat down at her new 'usual' spot, a table for four in the far corner. It sat next to the most unappealing water fountain in history. The spigot was plastered with wads of multi-colored bubble gum, and rust stains covered anything that might have once been metal, but it offered seclusion.

Opening her yogurt, Sandy scanned the crowd, looking for Adam. She saw him emerge from the cafeteria line with a tray. He was heading her way. She gently placed her spoon on a napkin, her appetite suddenly gone.

Adam strode with certainty toward her table, but as he neared, he became hesitant. He shyly asked, "Can I sit down?"

"Be my guest," Sandy replied curtly.

Adam sat in the chair across from her, leaned forward, and quietly asked, "Did you read my note? I'm ready to help in any way I can--no matter what you decide to do."

Sandy's face flushed with anger. "Are you kidding," she hissed. "You can't help in any way that really matters...not anymore." Sandy knew she wasn't being fair to Adam. He hadn't done anything to her, but she needed to be mad at someone. She instantly regretted her harsh words when she saw Adam's face collapse.

"I'm so sorry. I had no idea what was happening. If I'd known, I would have done something. You have to believe that." Desperation and guilt strangled his words, and tears threatened to spill from his eyes.

Sandy looked away remorsefully. "I guess I do believe you, and I know I shouldn't snap at you. I'm just so angry." She clenched her fists tightly and hid them under the table. "I just want to hit something."

"I hate my brother for what he did to you. That's why I'm here," Adam explained. He looked down at the table, afraid to make eye contact and mumbled, "I told my father, but..."

"You told your father? I didn't say you could tell anyone." A few students swung their heads around as Sandy's voice became shrill. "How dare you!" she seethed. She pushed abruptly away from the table and stood angrily.

"Wait...sit down." Adam patted the table and moved so he could sit beside her.

Sandy looked around her and noticed the curious stares. She sat back down, feeling even more embarrassed. The last thing she wanted was to draw attention to herself.

"I didn't tell him your name or anything. I just showed him the drugs I found in Justin's room and told him how he'd used them to...you know..." Adam trailed off. "I thought Dad would do something. I really did because this is serious shit this time. This isn't just a little pot or booze. This is..." He fought to find the right word. He sighed deeply and muttered, "It's insanity." He looked into Sandy's eyes, ashamed at his next words. "But, he didn't do anything. He took away Justin's car and flushed the pills. That's all he did. I've been at Ryan's house for the past two days because I can't stand to be around anyone in my family."

Sandy's eyes glittered with contempt. "I guess your dad doesn't want to ruin that big-bad rep he's got," Sandy said spitefully. "My uncle told me he was a dickhead, but to do absolutely nothing when you know your son is a monster... that's so messed up." Her breath caught as she stammered, "I guess my life just isn't that important, is it?" She turned to the wall and Adam watched as tears streamed down her face.

He touched her hand. "Justin *is* a monster. That's why I want to help you. He's not going to stop just because daddy slapped him on the wrist. *We* have to stop him. I'm able to back up your story. It won't be your word against his."

Sandy sniffed and blew her nose into a napkin. She felt utterly worthless. Her life was flipped upside down in one brief moment, and Adam expected her to tell everyone how stupid she was. She closed her eyes and began shaking her head from side to side. "I'm not doing it. I can't tell. I'll be humiliated. My parents will hate me.

I'll be the laughingstock of the whole school," she argued in one breath. She opened her eyes and glanced around at the throng of students, then glared at Adam. "I'm not going to relive the whole thing in a courtroom and be made to look like the town bicycle." Her voice grew hard. "Think about it, Adam. Your dad flushed the pills. You don't even have those as evidence. There's just your word. Hell, I don't even remember what happened. Do you think that'll go over well in a court of law where your dad rules? He's not stupid, you know."

Sandy's fierce eyes suddenly rounded and a choked moan escaped her parted lips. Adam followed her bewildered gaze and saw his brother, his arm slung over Michele's bare shoulders. Her skimpy halter top and mini-skirt definitely did not fit the school's laughably-enforced dress code. Didn't she realize it was November? She held a table of football players spellbound as she pointed out the rose tattoo that snaked around her left hip and ended near her bellybutton.

"I guess the new girl is next," Adam said softly.

Michele leaned across the table and grabbed a French fry from the quarterback's tray. Justin moved behind her and began to hump the air behind her, crudely simulating sex. All the other players laughed raucously. She straightened up and twirled around but found only an innocent Justin. She looked questionably between the rowdy boys and Justin who were now exchanging high fives. She knew she had missed something but didn't want to appear foolish, so she smiled good-naturedly.

"She doesn't know what she's getting into," Adam whispered. "Don't you think we should warn her?"

A steel cage slammed around Sandy's heart. "It looks like she can take care of herself," she replied grimly as she watched Justin possessively guide Michele through the crowded lunchroom.

"I wouldn't be too sure of that." Adam couldn't help but notice that Michele's confidence had been replaced with a look of uncertainty.

*   *   *

"That was the best fried chicken I've ever had." Amber sighed contentedly as she patted her stomach. "Thank you, Mrs. Dufrane." She looked around the large eat-in kitchen and couldn't help but admire the quaint décor. There was a definite mix of old and new. A large cast-iron stove sat in the corner, providing most of the kitchen's heat while a bevy of cooking gadgetry cluttered the countertops. Blue checked curtains decorated the window above the sink. On the windowsill grew an array of fresh herbs, and the aroma of freshly-baked apple pie hung heavily in the air. Amber felt sated and happy.

"You need to remember to call me Nana. All of Jake's friends call me that." She winked at Amber as she whisked away her plate and headed toward the sink. "I hope you saved room for dessert," she called out hopefully over her shoulder.

Amber looked at Jake, patted her stomach, and shook her head. "Amber and I are both stuffed, Nana." Jake carried over the rest of the dirty dishes. "Do you want us to load the dishwasher while you and Papa eat some dessert?"

"Don't cut into that pie yet," Papa said as he stood and stretched. "I need to check on one of the cows that's about to calve. Why don't we all let some of this food settle and meet back here in a little while to eat dessert?"

"That sounds like a heck of a plan," Nana said as she shooed Jake out of her way. "Why don't you show Amber the baby pigs out in the barn? I'll clean up here." She clapped her hands together excitedly. "Then we can all watch *Wheel of Fortune* later."

Amber and Jake pulled on their jackets and walked toward the dilapidated barn. It was getting colder--more like winter, and their breath appeared as little puffs of smoke "We don't need to go inside if you don't want to. It's pretty disgusting in there. You'll probably get manure all over your sneakers."

"Aw, shucks," Amber drawled in a perfect southern accent, "you know *ah* just hate gettin' dirty." She jumped onto Jake's back, and the sound of central New York returned to her voice. "You can just give me a piggyback ride and save my new Nikes."

Jake pretended to stagger under her weight. "How much chicken did you eat?" he joked playfully.

"You did *not* just go there!" Amber giggled and kicked her sneakers against Jake's sides as if he were a horse. "Take me to see those piglets before I throw you in the manure pile."

Nana had just finished bringing some empty boxes down to the basement when she heard the door slam thirty minutes later. As she climbed the stairs, Amber's cheerful laugh rang out. She was glad that Jake had found such a nice girl and what a looker, too! "Is it cold out there?" Nana asked curiously as she emerged from the cellar door. "Look at the flushed cheeks on the both of you. Come on in and get warm." Nana ushered them into the living room and pointed to the couch.

Jake looked at Amber and grinned, embarrassed. It *was* a bit chilly outside, but their blushes had more to do with the passionate kisses they exchanged while Papa was out of sight.

As soon as he sat down, Jake noticed his mother's senior picture prominently displayed on the mantel. He looked around breathlessly and noticed more pictures, photos he'd never seen before. He stood and wandered to the bookshelf where he found a small photograph of his mother and himself on a playground. He couldn't have been more than four, and she was pushing him on a swing.

Amber moved behind him and looked over his shoulder. "Is that you and your mom?" she inquired softly.

Jake nodded numbly and reached for another picture on an end table. It was of a little girl wearing one of those pointed cardboard birthday hats. She did not look happy, yet she held up a new doll for everyone to see. The torn and discarded wrapping paper made a small mountain at her feet.

"That's your mom at her third birthday party," Nana said as she stood next to Jake. She took the photograph from him and stared at it. "See how grumpy she looks? It's because I forced her to wear a dress for her party. She was such a tom-boy." Nana beamed and put the picture down. She moved to another frame and picked it up, showing Amber and Jake. "This was taken when your mom was sixteen. This was right after Papa had taken her for her first driving lesson. You should have seen your grandfather when they returned home. I thought he'd had a heart attack. He was so pale, and he wouldn't speak for a good thirty minutes. I had to take her driving after that. Apparently driving a tractor at five miles per hour across a wide open field didn't quite prepare Elizabeth, or your Papa, for highway speeds." Nana moved from picture to picture, explaining their significance to Jake and Amber. She didn't hear her husband come in the back door. He stood in the doorway to the living room and smiled as memories crowded the room.

"I finally decided, with a little help from your grandpa, that there's no need to keep Elizabeth boxed up." She put her arm around Jake, and they both turned so they were facing Elizabeth's graduation picture. "We will keep her alive with our memories and stories." Nana sniffed and Papa took two steps toward her until she waved him off. "I'm fine. It's just a little dusty in here, that's all. Now…who's ready for some pie and Pat Sajak? I know I am." Nana disappeared into the kitchen where she bustled about to serve up warm apple pie and creamy vanilla ice cream.

Jake turned the television to the correct channel and led Amber to the couch. He waved his hand around at the pictures. "This is like a little miracle," he said as he spun her toward him into an embrace. When he leaned down to kiss her lips, his cheeks glowed from happiness. Smiles graced everyone's faces that night, and Nana's famous apple pie had never tasted so good.

*   *   *

"Are you sure you don't want me to go in with you?" Ryan asked as Adam climbed out of the passenger side of his car.

"That's okay. I'll just be a few minutes," Adam replied. He'd returned home to pick up some more clothes. He wasn't sure how long he'd be staying at Ryan's, but he knew he was in no hurry to leave the relative sanity of the Chapin household.

"I'm going to go get some gas then; I'll be back in about ten minutes," Ryan said.

Adam gave him a thumbs-up and walked slowly toward the house. Even though his father's and Julia's vehicles were parked in the driveway, he didn't see or hear them when he opened the front door. Moving stealthily through the house and to his bedroom, he encountered no one. He wasn't exactly trying to sneak in and out of his house, but he'd decided it would make everything easier if he didn't encounter his father. He wouldn't have to invent any reasons for why he was staying at Ryan's house, and, most importantly, he wouldn't have to pretend to have even an ounce of respect for the man. There was nothing to say to him, and Adam wasn't sure if he could look upon his father with anything but disgust.

Adam moved quickly, stuffing underwear, socks, jeans, and tee shirts into his duffel bag. His heart thudded against his ribcage—he felt like a thief. He entered his bathroom, tossed in a few other essentials, and was ready to leave. It had taken him only three

155

minutes. He decided he'd make an excellent cat burglar as he left his door the way he'd found it, slightly ajar.

As he passed Justin's closed bedroom door, he thought of Michele, the new girl who would most likely be Justin's newest conquest. He couldn't help but feel guilty. Adam listened at the door and glanced at his watch. It was 5:30. Football practice ended at five. Was Justin in his room or hanging out with his friends? Adam couldn't be sure because Justin had to rely on a friend for rides now that his car was taken away from him. Adam rapped loudly on the door. He'd think of some excuse if Justin answered, but there was no response.

He turned the knob slowly, pushed open the door, and glanced inside. Adam breathed a sigh of relief when he realized Justin was not there. He quickly crossed the room to the dresser and began rifling through the drawers. The small pill bottle Adam had previously discovered had been wedged among Justin's socks, but this time the bureau contained only clothing. Adam continued searching, his actions feverish. He needed to know if his brother had more of the date rape drug, but he was terrified of being caught. Justin's threat reared up in the back of Adam's mind. He looked under the mattress, in the nightstand, behind the bookshelf, and through Justin's desk. His actions were hurried, yet, at the same time, he was careful to put everything back the way he'd found it.

Adam was hunting through the closet when he heard it. His head snapped up; he was instantly alert. It was Justin's ring tone. Adam could hear him on the oak staircase. He had only seconds to hide. Adam quietly closed the closet door and slipped to the back corner where Justin's hamper gave him some cover. His heart thudded against his rib cage. If Justin opened his closet, he would, without a doubt, be discovered.

"Whassup, brotha'?" Justin said into his cell phone. Adam heard the bed creak as Justin flopped onto it. "I just bagged that Michele chick. You know what that means...add another point in my column." There was a pause, and Adam knew he was talking to their brother Charles. "I knew she was a skank the first time I saw her. You saw her pictures, right?" Justin laughed at whatever Charles said.

Adam felt sick when he realized that Justin had only had sex with Michele to get his "point." *What a great welcome she got,* Adam thought grimly. How would she react at school on Monday? Would she pretend that nothing happened, or would there be a public showdown in the cafeteria? Adam hoped for the latter.

"No," Justin continued, "she didn't put up a fight, so it wasn't necessary. All I'm saying is that you might need to pick up the pace because little brother is catching up. Next year I'll be at college where the sea is a lot deeper, and this fisherman is planning to mount more than a few fish."

Adam's fear dissipated as his anger and disgust grew.

"So, did you get that picture I texted you? Yeah, she's my newest objective, but I have to know if you think she's a two-pointer or not. I'm not going to bother with her if she only counts as one. Based solely on her picture, she should be a two, but when you

157

factor in all the other obstacles that surround her, it's really a no-brainer, don't you think?"

Even though he was only hearing one side of the conversation, it didn't take a genius to figure out they were discussing their competition.

Justin chuckled. "Deal. Your chemistry professor for my little angel. I'll have to pull out all the stops with this one. Anything goes, right, Chuck?"

Adam stayed hidden until he heard Justin go downstairs a few minutes after he hung up with Charles. He had to talk to Sandy again. Someone else was now in danger. But who? Who was Justin's "angel?"

*   *   *

Jake lay in bed unable to sleep. His digital clock glared at him, taunting him as the minutes ticked by. It was just after two in the morning. He'd tried reading, but that hadn't helped, so he finally rolled out of bed with an irritated grunt. After Amber had left at ten, he hadn't been able to shut down his brain. His mother's smile was there every time he closed his eyes. He pulled on the pair of sweatpants and tee shirt he'd discarded on the floor when he'd gone to bed and crept quietly down the stairs, attempting to avoid the squeakiest ones. Papa's snores could be heard clearly, even through his closed door.

Once he reached the kitchen, he sliced himself a piece of pie and poured a glass of milk and carried them to the table. Nothing was better than his grandmother's apple pie. He savored every bite and gulped down the rest of the milk. He quietly placed his dishes into the sink and headed into the living room so he could look at his mother's photos again.

He picked up her framed senior portrait, gathered up the smaller photos and carried them to the couch, turning on the lamp as he sat down. Carefully shuffling among the frames, he studied each one, noticing how his mother's smile was the same in every photograph. She had one dimple on her left cheek. Her hair had been lighter when she was young. He examined each photo and remembered the stories Nana had told earlier that evening. She looked so happy in every one. Well, maybe she wasn't so happy in her third birthday picture, but he couldn't blame her. No tom-boy in her right mind would want to wear a frilly dress.

Jake yawned. He suddenly felt very sleepy. For once, he was feeling content after thinking about his mother, not miserable. Even though she'd been reduced to memories and colored ink on glossy paper, she was still able to comfort her son. He started replacing the framed photos around the room, wishing a silent goodnight to each one.

As he returned her senior picture to the mantel over the fireplace, he noticed a tiny corner of paper coming loose from behind the glass. His brow furrowed with curiosity as he carried the frame closer to the light. The paper was yellowed slightly. He sat down on the couch, set the other photos on the coffee table, and removed the back of the 8 X 10 frame. It was a newspaper article. Its headline screamed at Jake: *Murder Shocks Middlebury Residents.*

He gasped and looked away quickly, afraid to read about his mother's grisly murder. He stood and paced the living room anxiously, the article trembling in his unsteady hands.

His Nana and Papa Dufrane had shielded him from the publicity by whisking him away to his aunt's house outside Albany. They had returned, of course, to pack up Jake's belongings and bring them to their house. He had been protected from everything once the initial police questioning was done. Jake had not had to step foot in that house again, and he was thankful. He'd had nightmares almost every night for the first year and had spent six months attending evening counseling sessions with a nice older woman who always ended their appointments by sharing a roll of Sweet Tarts with him.

He was hesitant now to read about the details he'd tried so hard to forget. It was bad enough to be haunted by occasional nightmares, but to read the cold, emotionless facts recorded by some faceless reporter? He wasn't sure if he could do it. He'd never read any reports or seen any news coverage of the murder. His grandparents had done a great job protecting him. That's why it was so easy to start over at their house. Very few people knew the truth, but now the facts were resting like an impassive granite stone in his hands.

Jake took a deep breath. Nine years had passed, and Jake was no longer a child. Maybe he was finally ready to face his past and all the small details and memories it brought with it. His project had already helped more than he would have ever believed, so maybe reading the article would finally bring him some closure. He sank back onto the edge of the couch and leaned forward, his elbows resting on his knees. Holding the paper firmly, he began to read.

Murder Shocks Middlebury Residents

The sleepy town of Middlebury, VT was rocked yesterday morning when police found Elizabeth Carver, 32, murdered in her home. A 911 call was made from the home at 8:52 Sunday morning by Jacob Carver, the victim's son, age 7. Elizabeth Carver was pronounced DOA by EMTs at 9:22 a.m.

The coroner's initial report indicated that the cause of death was massive blood loss due to multiple stab wounds. An autopsy will be performed later today at the crime lab in Waterbury. Preliminary reports indicate that Mrs. Carver was killed by her husband of nine years, Greg Carver, age 33.

The victim's son, who was home at the time of the attack, was rushed to Porter Medical Center. The hospital reported no injuries to the boy. He was, however, kept overnight for observation. He was being treated for shock.

Residents of this peaceful neighborhood are shocked at the savagery of the crime and gathered en masse to pray for the family. Mrs. Conti, a neighbor, called the family "very loving" and is stunned by Greg Carver's actions. "They appeared to be the perfect family," she added.

Greg Carver was rushed by ambulance to Porter Medical Center. According to police reports, Carver had cut his own throat with the apparent murder weapon when the police confronted him in his bedroom. Although the injury was serious, it was not life-threatening, and Carver is expected to be transported to the Addison County Jail no later than Thursday when he will be arraigned.

-

Stacey Ashley

Addison Press

Jake looked up slowly. He stared at the opposite wall, his eyes blank and unfocused. The news article trembled in his fingertips before it fluttered soundlessly to the worn rug, landing next to his bare feet. His father was *alive*? Fury swept through his body. His breaths came in short, punctuated bursts, and his heart pounded, creating a dissonant symphony that roared in his ears. He stood up angrily and strode toward the stairs, ready to confront his sleeping grandparents, but he stopped before he even reached the bottom step. How could they let him believe all these years that his father was dead? A sense of betrayal overwhelmed Jake. What else had they lied about? He needed to escape the house; he grabbed his wallet, cell phone, and truck keys off the kitchen counter and strode to the mudroom to put on his jacket. He thrust his feet into his filthy barn boots and didn't bother tying the laces.

An icy burst of wind met him when he opened the door. He thrust his hands into the gloves he kept in his jacket. Snow was definitely on its way. Hot tears gathered at the corners of Jake's eyes as he climbed into his truck. He pounded the steering wheel in anger and frustration. It was 2:47 a.m. according to the dashboard clock whose eerie glow gave Jake's features a sickly hue.

CHAPTER 13

Jake woke suddenly with a start. *Where am I?* He looked around, panic beginning to set in. Suddenly, everything came back to him: the ten years of lies, his father alive and, no doubt, in prison, the deceit, his late night escape. He turned on the engine to check the time. It was 5:10. The sun had not yet made her appearance, and Jake shivered in the cold air. The truck started, coughing and sputtering against the frigid temperature.

He hadn't known where he would go when he left his grandparent's house, so he'd driven around aimlessly until he realized he was near the gorge. He'd decided to pull into the parking area because there, at least, he could be surrounded by some good memories. Pitch blackness enveloped the truck, the moon and stars cloaked by dense clouds. Wrapped in tomblike silence, Jake's anger was soon replaced with a mind-numbing fatigue to which he surrendered gratefully.

A light snow had begun to fall while he slept, and now his windshield was dusted with it. The truck murmured soothingly as Jake warmed his hands with the hot air blasting from the heater. He didn't want to go home; he wanted answers. He certainly did not want to hear a bunch of excuses from either set of grandparents. Obviously, they'd woven this web of lies together. There was only one place for Jake to go. Now that he'd decided what to do, he felt better. He shifted into drive, pulled onto the main road, and headed toward Vermont where he hoped to find the truth.

*   *   *

Amber was awakened at eight by a light knocking on her bedroom door. "What?" she muttered sleepily. Spencer stirred under the covers but didn't emerge.

Her father's voice came through the door. "Sweetie, Jake's grandmother is on the phone and she'd like to speak to you. Can I come in?"

Amber sat up and rubbed the sleep out of her eyes. "Yeah...sure." She was slightly worried. Why would Nana be calling her so early on a Saturday?

Ben opened the door, handed Amber the phone and left, leaving the door slightly ajar.

"Hi, Nana. Is something wrong?" Amber asked hesitantly.

"Well, I'm not sure if something is wrong, but something sure isn't right, that's for sure." Nana could not hide her concern. "Have you seen Jake this morning?" she asked.

Amber could hear the hopeful tone of her question. "No," she replied, tossing off the covers and standing. "I haven't seen him since last night at your house. Is he in the barn or maybe in one of the fields?"

"No...in fact, his truck's not here, so we were hoping he was with you." Nana sighed heavily. "I just knew this would come back to bite us in the long run." Her anger and frustration were evident. "I guess we shouldn't have kept it from him for all these years," she mumbled.

"What are you talking about?" Amber asked, fully awake now. She was attempting to dress herself while still holding onto the phone. "What have you kept from him?" She cradled the phone between her head and shoulder and yanked on some jeans.

"Oh, dear, where to even start? Has Jake told you about his parents...not about the car accident but the *truth* about his parents?"

"Yes, he actually told me all about it last week. I hope you're not mad at him for confiding in me," Amber said uneasily as she pulled on some socks. "What a horrible thing for a seven year old to deal with."

Nana's voice softened. "No, I'm not mad at him. I'm glad that he found someone to trust. The problem is..." Nana paused, ashamed to admit this aloud. "We kept part of the truth hidden from Jake—a big part," she added in a whisper. She rushed to continue, "But, we only did it because we thought we were doing the right thing. At the time, it felt like the best thing to do, but now he's found out and I'm sure he's furious at us. We don't know where he is or what he might do." Nana's voice broke.

Amber's heart shattered to hear Nana so despondent. "Slow down, Nana. This isn't your fault. I'm sure he's safe." Amber tried to sound calm, but cold fear gripped her. Jake was missing! "I'll call Jake's friends. We'll find him. Don't worry," Amber said soothingly in an attempt to placate Nana and compose herself as well. "Nana, what did Jake find out?"

Nana blew her nose loudly and drew in a long, shuddering breath. "He found the news article I'd hidden. I'd forgotten all about it. I found it this morning on the floor, and some of Elizabeth's pictures were scattered all over the coffee table. It was inside one of the picture frames. Oh, how I wish I'd never taken out all those old photos." She started crying once again. Amber could barely make out her next words. "Jake's father only *tried* to kill himself. He's still alive."

"He's *what?*" Amber asked shocked. She sat heavily on her bed. She couldn't grasp what Nana had just said. If she was this stunned by the news, she couldn't fathom how Jake was handling it. He must be reeling.

"He's been in prison in Vermont this whole time," Nana was saying when Amber finally tuned back into the conversation. "The article says that the knife wound was not life threatening, so Jake knows Greg's alive. We keep calling his cell phone, but he won't answer. I guess I can't blame him. He must be so angry and confused right now. Can you think of anywhere he might have gone?" she asked expectantly.

"He might be at Ryan's or Adam's. I'll check to see if he's there. I'll call you back if I find out anything. Call me if he comes home, okay, Nana?"

"I will. Thank you, Amber. I'm glad he has a good friend like you."

*   *   *

Jake pulled into the tiny parking lot. He'd passed by this small, brick building numerous times while driving to Burlington with his grandparents. He was thankful now that he'd paid attention during

167

the long trips. The snow had stopped about an hour ago, and the sun was now shining brightly. Jake sat, gripping the steering wheel, his knuckles turning white. He was aware of everything around him: the ticking of the engine, the cold air invading the warm cab, the cacophony of geese flying overhead, and the empty feeling in the pit of his stomach.

Drops of water dripped from the roof as the snow melted. A woman entered the tiny building with a young child in tow, each carrying a small pile of books. Jake knew he could delay no longer. He took a deep breath, swung open the door of the truck, and walked with purpose into the Swanton Public Library, intent on discovering the truth.

A teenaged girl sat behind a circular desk reading a Stephen King novel. As Jake approached her, she held up one finger. Jake took one look at her and decided not to interrupt. Her hair was dyed dark purple and pulled back into a messy ponytail, three silver hoops adorned one eyebrow, a heavy ring in the shape of a snake twisted around her entire middle finger, and a black Metallica tee-shirt completed the look. He waited patiently at the desk and appreciated the artistry of her fingernails. They were polished in black and each was decorated with a white skull.

She finished her paragraph and placed the book upside down on the desk to save her place. "How can I help you?" she asked in a surprisingly friendly voice.

"Um...I'm looking for old newspaper articles." Jake had rehearsed his story many times during the drive. "I'm investigating an old murder that took place in Middlebury for my forensic science class."

"Really? We don't have interesting classes like that where I go. What school do you go to?" she asked.

Jake picked up on the girl's enthusiasm. He wasn't surprised by her interest in the macabre given her choice of novel and appearance. He couldn't have been any luckier. With her help, he'd have his answers in no time. "I go to school in upstate New York, but I was on my way to Burlington to visit family and decided to stop in here. I figured I'd get more help at a smaller library."

"Great. This will be fun. I usually just help old people or little kids. It's a pretty boring job, but it gives me time to read and do homework. My name's Becka," she said with a smile.

"I'm Matt." He felt a little bad about lying since she seemed so nice. The two shook hands.

"Okay, Matt, follow me." Becka led him through a maze of bookcases and down some stairs.

Jake followed her bouncing ponytail. When she stopped abruptly next to a large machine, Jake almost walked on her heels. "Sorry," Jake said embarrassed.

Becka laughed. "No prob." She pointed to the machine. "This cumbersome relic," she said with a flourish, "is a microfilm machine. We'll have to use this thing to find what you're looking for." She turned toward Jake. "You said this was an old murder. How old are we talking here?" she asked, all businesslike.

"The murder occurred in August of 2003," Jake replied.

"That's not that old," Becka said a little disappointed. "But, we'll still have to check out the microfilm because *The Burlington Free Press* doesn't go that far back in its online archives." She patted the light blue contraption and walked toward a wall of metal filing cabinets. She scanned the front of each drawer, looking for the correct section. She glanced over her shoulder at Jake. "We don't carry microfilm for the smaller papers, but I'm sure the Burlington paper covered the story. Murder is always big news, especially when it happens in a small town." She faced the cabinets once again. "Aha...here it is," she said enthusiastically. She pulled out a small cardboard box and held it up triumphantly. "This contains all the articles for July through September."

"In that tiny box?" Jake asked dubiously. "It's not very big."

"I take it you've never used a microfilm reader, have you?" Becka poured the contents of the box into her hand. She held it up for Jake to see.

"It looks like one of those old movie reels except in miniature," Jake said as he took the reel from Becka.

"I'll show you how to load it, and then I'd better get back to the desk. Come get me if you need help, though." Becka showed Jake how to place the reel onto the spindle. "You just feed the film through here and it will collect onto the empty reel on the other side." Her hands moved swiftly and assuredly. "Push the tray in and turn on the lamp. It's as easy as that." She pointed to a large knob. "Turn this knob to advance to the day you're looking for. It moves really fast, so stop every now and then and check the date on the

170

paper. Obviously, it goes in chronological order. Are you all set?" she asked.

The instructions stampeded through Jake's brain. "I think I've got it," he said dubiously. "I'll come get you if I need some help. Thanks, Becka."

She turned to go as Jake sat on the stool. "I'll take care of the microfilm when you're done. Just tell me when you're leaving, okay?"

"Sure thing," Jake responded. He watched her walk away until he heard her footsteps echo on the stairs. He swung back toward the machine. His heart was like a runaway train. He was sure Becka had heard it pounding. He turned the knob to the right. Images sped across the machine. He stopped and the images came to an abrupt standstill. He searched for the date. July 18th. He spun the knob again and again until he got to August 12th, the day after the murder. There it was—front page news—the article detailing the horror of that day. He read it carefully but didn't learn anything new. The information was the same as what he'd read in *The Addison Press*.

He advanced through the pages, scanning for additional information. The follow-up articles he discovered were quite extensive. The initial story had created an influx in human interest pieces. He read one entitled "The Monster Next Door" in which several of his parent's neighbors had been interviewed. They all said the same thing. "They seemed like the perfect family." His mother's photos accompanied articles about the rise in domestic violence, but he was most startled when he saw a picture of himself. That day,

171

someone had taken a picture of him wrapped in the arms of a police officer. One arm was wound tightly around the officer's neck while the other stretched piteously toward the house. Jake could read the agony on his younger self's crumpled face. He stared at that picture until a loud sneeze from the other room broke his trance.

He spun the knob again, looking for information about a trial. Finding nothing, Jake made his way back to the microfilm drawer and found the box labeled September-December. He managed to load the microfilm and spooled almost all the way to the end of the reel before he finally found what he was looking for. When he finally found it, he read carefully. It was an open and shut case, so the trial had been swift. The police had everything they needed to put Greg Carver away for a very long time: his fingerprints on the murder weapon, his wife's blood splattered on the clothes he'd worn, a statement from the only witness, his own son, and his feeble suicide attempt. Carver had never taken the stand in his defense and had never offered up a motive. The jurors deliberated for only one hour before Greg was sentenced to life in prison at the Northern State Correctional Facility in Newport, Vermont.

Jake's stomach twisted crazily, and his head began to ache. It was surreal to find the most horrifying event of his life reduced to tiny black print. There was no emotion in the reporter's directness; he was only reporting the facts.

Jake rubbed his eyes and pushed his stool away from the screen. He was slightly disappointed in his search; he'd been hoping to read about a motive, but there was nothing. There was no answer

172

to the question Jake sought. As he glanced once again at the screen, he knew what he would have to do. Jake snagged a square of scrap paper from the pile on the table and jotted down the pertinent information. He turned off the machine and climbed the stairs.

Newport wasn't far from Swanton, but he needed some directions. "I'm all done with the microfilm. I turned off the reader but left the film inside. Is that all right?" Jake asked Becka who was back to reading her novel.

"Sure, that's fine. Did you find what you were looking for?" she asked curiously.

"I did, but I need to look up some stuff on the Internet. Is there a computer I can use?"

"Right through that doorway," Becka directed, pointing over her left shoulder.

It took Jake about five minutes to find a phone number and driving directions to the prison. It would only take him an hour and a half to get there. Maybe, just maybe, he'd finally get an answer to the one question that had haunted him all these years. Why did his father do it? There had to be a reason.

He started up the truck so it could warm up and pulled out his cell phone. A flurry of missed calls and voicemail messages assailed him, but he wasn't interested in talking to anyone. He didn't need his grandparents trying to convince him to go home. Instead, he dialed the phone number scrawled on the crumpled piece of paper. Even in the cold, the paper grew damp from his sweaty hands. The phone rang twice before someone answered. "Hi. My name is Jake Carver. I'd like to know if a Greg Carver is still incarcerated there."

*   *   *

"Sandy, I know you have your reasons for not reporting Justin. Believe me, I understand, but you've got to hear me out," Adam pleaded. He sat in the hallway outside Ryan's bedroom, leaning against the wall, his knees pulled to his chest. Even though it was 9:30, Ryan still slept soundly. Adam had been awakened at eight by the intermittent snores erupting from Ryan's side of the room. Every time Adam had fallen back to sleep, he'd been startled awake by the blasts emanating from Ryan's throat. He'd finally given up and decided to call Sandy from his cell phone.

"You're not going to convince me to humiliate myself, you know," she responded dryly.

"Maybe I won't have to convince you after you hear what I have to say. Maybe you'll just decide on your own." Adam continued before Sandy had a chance to argue. "I snuck into Justin's room yesterday and went through his drawers. That's where I found the pills the last time."

"Did you find anything?" Sandy interrupted.

"No. I looked around a few other places too, but I found nothing."

He heard Sandy sigh heavily. "So, why are you calling me?" she asked, frustration flooding her words.

"I'm getting to that part," he responded calmly. "I heard Justin's phone ring on the stairs and barely had time to hide. I overheard him talking to our brother Charles about their stupid contest."

"Whoa—what stupid contest?" Sandy interjected angrily.

Adam looked up at the ceiling. How was he supposed to explain to Sandy that she'd been merely a pawn in a sick game? "My brothers are sick and I'm nothing like them. I want you to understand that."

"What is this contest?" she asked, seething with malice.

Adam decided to get this over with quickly. "They're trying to see who can have sex with the most girls before they hit 21, and, apparently, they'll do whatever it takes to win."

It took Sandy a few seconds to process what Adam told her. She felt instantly nauseous and ran to the bathroom, afraid she would throw up. "What the fuck is wrong with them?" she shrieked into the phone before she hung up.

Adam stared at the phone in his hand as the dial tone droned accusingly. He pushed the 'end' button; helplessness threatened to swallow him. He leaned his head against the wall feeling totally powerless. Without warning, the phone vibrated in his hand. Shocked, he dropped it and watched it fall with a soft thud onto the carpet. He gathered it up quickly and answered. It was Sandy. Relief swept through him.

"Finish what you were going to tell me," she said. "It certainly can't get any worse."

Adam could hear the sadness in her voice, but he could also detect anger. Anger was good. It meant she hadn't given up. He told

175

her everything he'd overheard about Michele and about Justin's newest objective. "I don't know who this "angel" could be, but she's worth two points. He said something about how the obstacles surrounding her would make her a difficult conquest. He also said he was going to stop at nothing to get her."

"A point system? Do you know how twisted that is?" Sandy asked. She fought back tears as she thought of herself reduced from a person to a point. And she was certain she'd been worth only a point. "Your brothers are the biggest prick bastards on the planet. Do you know where I went after school yesterday? To the clinic to be tested. Do you know how embarrassing that was? A woman my mom bowls with works there," she croaked. She swallowed hard, determined not to cry. "What am I going to do if he gave me some disease, Adam?"

"This is why I want you to go to the police with me. We have to stop him. How will you feel knowing he's done this to some other unsuspecting girl? I'll tell you how I feel." Adam's voice grew louder with his conviction. "I feel like absolute dog shit that I didn't listen to my gut the first time I saw a girl leaving our house in tears. Maybe if I'd said something then, nothing would have happened to you." Adam's speech was interrupted by Ryan opening the door.

"Are you all right, chief?" he asked curiously.

Adam covered the mouthpiece with his hand. "I'm fine. I'm talking to Sandy." He waved Ryan away so he could continue his conversation. Ryan backed into his room and closed the door.

"Are you still at Ryan's house?" Sandy asked.

176

"Yeah. I don't want to go back home. Would you go if you were me?"

"No way. Your house is for crazy people." Sandy's voice got low. "Are you afraid of him too?"

Adam considered his answer then decided to be honest. "Yes, I am. That's why I'm staying here." Adam switched the phone to his other ear. "Sandy, I need you to make a decision either way because I need to do something. If you don't want to get involved, I won't hold it against you."

"Let me think about it, okay, Adam. I'll call back this afternoon. I just want it to be something I can live with too."

"That sounds fair. I'll be waiting for your call. Bye, Sandy."

*   *   *

Amber pulled into her driveway, feeling utterly useless. She'd been driving around town looking for Jake's truck, but she'd had no luck. She'd hoped to see his truck in the school's parking lot, figuring he'd want to expend his pent-up energy by going for a run through the nature trails behind the school. She'd driven past Ryan and Adam's houses, but she wasn't surprised when his truck wasn't parked in either of their driveways. After all, they both thought Jake's parents had died in a car crash. It would be too difficult for Jake to explain everything to them.

She knew inherently that he'd gone somewhere to be alone with his thoughts and memories, so she'd driven to the gorge. The parking area had been, disappointingly, empty. Normally, Amber would have appreciated the beauty of the two inches of white snow that enveloped the lot, but that morning, it had felt like a bleak, barren wasteland.

Now, an hour and a half later, Amber felt miserable. Why hadn't Jake called her? Why had he run away like that? As she trudged up the stairs to the porch, she wondered what to do. She'd never felt so helpless. "I'm back," she called out as she entered the house and began untying her boots. Spencer raced toward her, barking noisily. He jumped against her legs in an attempt to plaster her face in sloppy kisses. Amber gently pushed him away. "Yuck, Spencer, your mouths smells like death with a side of rotten lobster. What have you been eating?" She threw Spencer a Breath Buster dog treat and walked into the kitchen. She found a note on the kitchen table written in her mom's elegant handwriting telling her that her parents and sisters had gone to the mall and to a movie.

Great, she thought to herself. She'd decided on her drive home that she was going to tell her parents about Jake's past and this morning's disappearance. She was all out of ideas; she needed their advice. After Nana's call that morning, she'd told her parents that Nana needed help with something. Even telling that small lie had made her feel guilty, but she didn't feel right telling her family about a secret Jake had kept from even his best friends. Now, he'd stumbled upon another secret, a huge secret, and he had no one. All of her calls to his cell had gone directly to voicemail.

She picked up the cordless phone and dialed. "Hi, Nana—it's Amber. Have you heard from Jake?"

"Not a word," she replied. "I'm guessing from your question that you couldn't find him either."

"No. I drove all around town and out to the gorge, but I didn't see his truck anywhere." Amber sat at the kitchen table. "I didn't call Ryan or Adam because they still think that Jake's parents died in a car accident. I did drive by to see if he was there, though. Nana, if I ask for their help, I'm going to have to tell them the truth." Amber rested her forehead in her palm. "I don't know where else to look and they might have some ideas. Do you think Jake will hate me if I tell them?"

"I'm more interested in finding Jake," Nana said bluntly. "I vote for telling them. They are good boys and will understand. Besides, Jake is going to be so mad at us he won't have any anger left in him for you, honey. I wish he'd just answer his cell phone and scream at me. I just want to know that he's all right." Nana's worry weighed heavily upon her. For all these years, she'd thought she'd done the right thing by protecting Jake against the truth, but now she knew she was wrong, and it was much too late to change things.

Amber hung up the phone a few minutes later and dialed Adam's home phone, but no one answered. She had to look up Ryan's number since she never actually believed she'd ever be dialing it. "Hey, Ryan, it's Amber," she said quickly, steeling herself for some smartass comments.

Ryan was shocked; Amber was the last person he'd expect to call him. He looked over at Adam who was busily shoveling Captain Crunch into his mouth. "Whoa, Adam, the dyke's calling me. She must be sick of Jake and craving a real man...one with some meat on his bones."

Amber rolled her eyes at Ryan's immaturity, but she was glad to find out that Adam was there. Now she wouldn't have to speak to this moron. "Listen, dipshit," she growled menacingly, "just put Adam on the phone."

"Man, is there ever a time when you're *not* on the rag?" he asked contemptuously. He tossed the phone to Adam who still held his spoon halfway to his mouth. The phone hit the table with a bang and fell to the floor.

"Sorry, Amber," Adam said sheepishly. "I dropped the phone." He looked angrily at Ryan. "I wasn't exactly expecting a phone to come flying at me out of nowhere." Ryan's retort was cut short as Adam made his way into another room.

"I simply cannot talk to that d-bag. He's such an ass," Amber said angrily.

"He's really not all that bad," Adam replied. "He's actually been helping me out with something recently. It's all just a show. Trust me, Amber. Ryan Chapin is actually capable of being *nice*."

"I guess I'll have to take your word for it," Amber said. An awkward silence ensued.

"Ummmm, so what's up?" Adam asked hesitantly.

"Jake's missing," Amber blurted out.

"What?" Adam asked incredulously. He sank onto the couch in the living room. "What do you mean missing?"

Ryan appeared in the doorway. "Who's missing?"

180

Adam waved dismissively at him. "For how long?"

"Nana called me this morning at around eight. She's not sure when he left, but she knows he was very upset about something. She asked me to drive around, but I couldn't find him anywhere. I told her I'd call the two of you to see if you guys had any ideas. So…do you have any ideas?" she asked hopefully. Amber heard Adam relay their conversation to Ryan.

Ryan reached for the phone, and Adam handed it over submissively. "Is he, like, really missing or is Nana worrying over nothing? He hasn't been gone that long."

"Use your feeble little brain, Ryan," Amber replied angrily. "When is the last time Jake just left his grandparent's house without leaving a note? I'm sure the answer is never, so stop acting like a first-class dickwad." Amber's face was hot with anger. "He's not with *us*, so where is he, Einstein?"

"How the hell do I know? Did she tell you why he got so upset? That would probably be a helpful clue, Dr. Twatson."

"Dr. Twatson?" Amber smiled into the phone. "Okay—that was a good one; I'll give you that."

"Thanks," Ryan said happily. "Sometimes I even surprise myself."

Amber sighed heavily. "Look, it's a long story. Can we all just meet up somewhere? I'll tell you everything; then we can make a plan. Trust me…she has a reason to be worried." Amber tapped her foot impatiently, listening to their muffled conversation.

Ryan responded. "We were heading to Adam's house in a little while, so meet us there at ten."

A loud click sounded in Amber's ear as Ryan abruptly hung up the phone. She looked over at the clock on the microwave. She had about twenty-five minutes. Since Adam only lived a mile away, she had some time to kill. "C'mon, Spencer, let's tire you out with some fetch." After only ten minutes, Amber had to carry an exhausted Spencer back into the house where he flopped onto his dog bed and promptly began snoring. It was still too early to leave, but Amber was restless with inactivity. She wrote her parents a quick note, grabbed her car keys, and headed out the door.

CHAPTER 14

Amber had been sitting in the Krovlovskis' driveway for five minutes. It was almost ten, and Adam's father had hurriedly left a few minutes before, his Escalade coming dangerously close to crashing into her car. He hadn't even acknowledged her with a wave, not that she'd ever expect him to. Men like Blake Krovlovski did not notice other people; they were only concerned with themselves.

As the frigid air crept into Amber's car, she shivered. *Why am I sitting out here in the cold?* she asked herself. She patted her pocket to check for her phone, zipped up her jacket, and pushed open the car door. She glanced about, appreciating the wintry scene and wishing Jake were there to admire it with her. The sky was a bright blue, and the sun shone brightly, adorning the newly fallen snow with sparkling diamonds. A blue jay swooped back and forth from a nearby maple tree to an elaborate birdhouse. Amber followed Mr. Krovlovski's tracks to the back door, her boots crunching against the snow. The first snowfall of the year was always a thing of beauty, but after a few storms and lots of shoveling, the novelty of it quickly wore off.

Amber rang the doorbell, blowing into her hands in an attempt to warm them. She realized that she would need to unearth her gloves, scarf, and toque when she returned home. Julia, Adam's stepmother, answered the door and waved her inside. She was talking on her cell phone. Amber stamped her boots against the steps in an effort to remove some of the snow before she entered. Julia pointed one perfectly manicured finger into the air to indicate that she'd be off the phone momentarily. She disappeared into the adjoining room and her voice became muffled, but the conversation still had an air of intensity about it. Amber pulled off her boots and set them on the rug next to the door before sitting down at the long kitchen table. She doubted the Krovlovskis ever sat down together at this table to eat as a family. Adam had told her enough stories for her to know that these people were not the Brady Bunch type. She fiddled absently with the salt and pepper shakers and kept eyeing the digital clock on the microwave. It was now 9:54.

Suddenly, Julia appeared, dressed in a calf-length black winter coat. She appeared startled when she saw Amber sitting there, like she didn't remember inviting her in only minutes before. She stopped dead in her tracks. "Oh," she said, "I forgot that you were here." She pulled on her black leather gloves and looked at Amber, closely now, her head titled to one side. "You're one of Adam's little friends, right?" she cooed.

Amber ignored Julia's patronizing tone. She smiled and nodded. "Yes, I am. Good memory," she praised. Two could play at this little game. "I'm Amber. Adam told me to meet him here at ten."

Julia glanced at her very expensive gold watch. "It's almost ten now. I'm sure he'll be here soon. I can't imagine him keeping a beautiful girl like you waiting for long," she said conspiratorially with a wink. The condescending tone was gone now.

They were suddenly just two gals. It was enough to make Amber sick. She watched as Julia pulled some lipstick out of her purse and applied it over her already berry-red lips. Amber plastered a false smile onto her face. "Mrs. Krovlovski, I can see you've got somewhere to go. I can wait in my car," Amber said standing. "I don't want to make you late now, do I?" Her smile stretched into a wide grin as though she and Julia shared a secret. She pushed in her chair and took a few steps toward the door.

"Don't be silly, Amber. I'm sure Adam will be here any second. You can wait here in the kitchen, but maybe you'll be more comfortable watching TV in the living room. Go ahead and make yourself at home." She smiled reassuringly as she gestured toward the living room where a giant flat-screen TV awaited. After zipping up a pair of black leather boots that would make a hooker blush, Julia moved quickly for the door leading to the garage. The heels of her boots click-clacked against the stone floor, creating a staccato gunfire that made Amber wince. "Bye, Amber," she called out sweetly over her shoulder.

Amber stood uncomfortably in the kitchen. She wasn't sure what to do or where to wait; it was strange to be left alone in someone else's house. The roar of Julia's car interrupted Amber's thoughts, and she glanced out the window in time to see her swing out of the driveway. She was certain Julia's haste was due to some sort of "date." Poor Adam—his stepmother's extracurricular activities made for interesting discussions among the town gossips. Nothing was secret in a small town. It was a mystery as to why Blake didn't divorce her. Maybe he was worried about paying

185

alimony, or perhaps they had an open relationship. What was certain was that no one would dare ask him.

Amber looked at the clock once again and decided to do what Julia had said—make herself at home. The lush carpet in the living room felt like a cloud compared to the cold stone tiles in the kitchen. She studied the room, taking in the design and how it differed from her own living room. There was an obvious absence of family photos. Instead, oversized paintings in ancient gilt frames adorned the walls. A mix of modern furniture and antiques crowded the room. Everything was dark—the walls, the wood, the furniture—and masculine. There really weren't any feminine touches in the room. No paisley prints, no fresh (or fake) flowers, and no pretty throw pillows decorated the room. Amber took off her jacket, laid it neatly over the arm of the enormous dark-brown leather couch and turned on MTV.

*   *   *

A buzzing droned in Justin's ear. He rolled over in bed and fumbled with his alarm clock. The irksome hum continued until he realized it was his cell phone. He groped blindly for it on his nightstand. Finally, he sat up, seized his phone and irritably answered, "This better be important."

"Justin, it's Julia," she began cheerily. "I hit a detour a few minutes ago because of an accident."

"You woke me up to tell me that! What do I care?" Justin did not hide his dislike for Julia. Even though she was a hot piece of ass, she was also a total slut and playing his father for a fool. He was about to hang up when he heard his stepmother's voice; the sweet tone was gone now.

"Look," she continued matter-of-factly, "I left one of Adam's friends in the kitchen—the cute blonde—and I'm assuming he's caught up in this accident since he wasn't there when I left. I don't think your brother would keep *that* girl waiting. Anyway, I was just thinking you could keep her company since Adam might not be home for awhile. You know what I mean…make sure she doesn't steal anything," she added bluntly.

Justin threw his covers aside and stood beside the bed. "Is her name Amber?" he asked nonchalantly, but his mind was spinning.

"That's her," Julia chirped, happy once again. She knew Justin would get downstairs as quickly as his horny little self could carry him. *Men are such predictable creatures*, she mused.

"Don't worry; I'll keep her company," Justin said sweetly, already pulling on some clothes. He slid shut his phone with finality. *The possibilities*, he thought as he entered his walk-in closet. He hurriedly pushed aside the shirts and pants hanging in his way until he found it. The gray suit looked innocent enough, but the right breast pocket held something altogether malevolent, and Justin knew right where to find it.

Amber turned when she heard someone coming down the stairs. She'd forgotten about the possibility of Justin being home and was now self-conscious as she sat in his living room as though she owned the place. "Oh, hi, Justin. I'm waiting for Adam," she said by means of explanation.

"So that's what brings you by so early on a Saturday morning. And here I thought you might be here to see me," he said coyly with a wink. He continued into the kitchen.

That was a short conversation, Amber thought. She settled back onto the couch. She could hear Justin rummaging around in the kitchen. He returned a few moments later with two glasses of orange juice. He set one on a coaster before her and took two big gulps of his own, his Adam's apple bobbing with each swallow.

"What are your plans today?" he asked as he settled into the matching leather armchair.

Amber took a long drink of her juice, stalling for time. She certainly didn't want to explain Jake's disappearance to Justin. "Oh, not much. I was supposed to meet Adam and Ryan here at ten o'clock, but apparently Ryan doesn't know how to tell time." She took another swig and placed the empty glass back onto the coaster. She felt awkward around Justin. They'd never had a conversation before, and now here they were--all alone. They watched a few minutes of a stupid reality show before, thankfully, a commercial interrupted a bar fight between two scantily-clad women. Amber glanced over at Justin as a ringtone advertisement filled the screen. Her mind whirled as she fought to fill the uncomfortable silence with small talk. "Have you filled out your college applications yet?"

Justin tore his gaze away from the television. Unlike Amber, he was extremely at ease. "Of course. I'm always way ahead of the game. I've always believed that when I want something badly enough, I'm going to take it. Nothing will stand in my way." He smiled at Amber. "I really want to go to Syracuse. Didn't your dad coach there?"

"Yes, he did—for thirteen years," she stammered. She suddenly wasn't feeling well. A trickle of sweat skated between her breasts. Her hands and face felt clammy, and she could feel the loose tendrils of her hair sticking to the nape of her neck. She glanced from Justin back to the TV. Her head felt suddenly very heavy. Her vision swam and dizziness rolled over her. Her tongue felt thick and dry. Everything was blurry as though she were looking through her mother's prescription glasses. An icy wave rolled over her, and she shivered, hugging her arms around herself. She knew in the pit of her stomach that something was deeply wrong. She shook her head in an attempt to clear it. Her voice was frozen, and Justin was looking at her curiously. Was that her phone ringing? She groped blindly, intent on finding it, but her movements were too slow. Too late...too late...the Cheshire cat approached her and pulled her fumbling hands away. He brushed her hair away from her eyes, and the ringing was silenced. She felt his arms wrap her in danger before everything faded to black.

*   *   *

Ryan slammed shut the car door in annoyance. "Stupid ass kids," he mumbled as he turned the car's heater on full-blast and held his hands over the vents.

"You're a stupid-ass kid," Adam pointed out logically. The two had been stuck in a line of cars for fifteen minutes before Ryan had finally gone to investigate. "So, what's the scoop?"

"Some idiotic kids from Franklin Academy caused a three-car accident. One car's already been moved to the side, but the other two are hooked together somehow and blocking the road, so we have to wait for the cops and a tow truck."

Volunteer firemen had been steadily arriving for the last few minutes. The lights on their pickup trucks flashed blue and white. They drove on the wrong side of the road, determined to get as close as possible to the crash site. Turning around to find an alternate route would have to wait until emergency personnel stopped arriving. An ambulance siren could be heard in the distance. "How close did you get? Could you tell if anyone was seriously injured?" Adam asked, concerned. "Did you recognize any of the vehicles?"

"I was close enough," Ryan replied, "to see a pretty nice car one hundred percent totaled. Do you remember that Jon kid who was in our study hall last year?" Ryan noticed Adam's blank look and continued. "He was the big guy who always wore shit-covered boots and gave the hall monitors a hard time."

"Okay, I remember him. Isn't he the redneck who broke his friend's eye socket after the prom?" Adam turned down the heater as soon as Ryan looked away.

"That's the guy," Ryan said. "He's up there stopping traffic and directing the emergency vehicles. Apparently, they'll let just about anyone be a volunteer fireman. Anyway, he's the one who said the kids caused the accident. They slid on the snow and sideswiped a car with an older couple inside." Ryan leaned over and blasted the heat once again.

190

"Did the older people get hurt?" Adam could see the kaleidoscope of lights from the ambulance ahead.

"I don't think so, but they're probably going to get checked out at the hospital anyway. Old people are brittle, you know."

Adam reached over to adjust the heat once again, but Ryan smacked his hand. "We're in *my* car. Go for a walk if you're too hot," he replied grumpily.

"What the hell is your problem?" Adam asked, annoyed. "It's not like you were in an accident."

"Dude, it's 10:15. Amber's waiting at your house, and I'm sure she's not going to be too happy when she sees us." Ryan looked over his left shoulder and wondered if he'd be able to make a U-turn, but he saw another set of emergency lights headed his way.

Adam reached into his jeans pocket and withdrew his phone. He dialed Amber's number to explain why they were late. "She's not answering. I wonder if she left her phone in her car," Adam said to Ryan as an automated voice instructed him to leave a message at the tone. "Amber, it's Adam. There was an accident near Carly's Café and the road's blocked. Call me when you get this message." He shoved the phone back into his pocket.

*　　*　　*

Jake's heart raced as he climbed out of the truck and stared at the massive building before him. It was hard to describe what he was feeling. There was dread, certainly, but he also felt fear, anger, and a hint of excitement. He was doing precisely what no one wanted him to do. As he made his way to the clearly marked visitors' entrance, he was struck, suddenly, with the reality of the situation. He was about to see his father, the man who had killed his mother for no reason at all. He wavered slightly, hesitating before the heavy glass door. *Am I really ready for this?* he wondered silently.

His hand gripped the cold metal of the door handle with more courage than he actually felt. He pulled open the door and walked inside, ready to face the man who'd robbed him of everything. He needed to know why his father had done it and what had made him snap. There was no way Jake was going to turn back now. As an iron cage closed around his heart, Jake calmly walked toward the man in uniform seated at the check-in desk.

The man looked up from his paperwork as Jake approached. "Visiting hours haven't started yet," he said, boredom evident in his tone.

"I've never been here before," Jake stammered. "I just found out that…"

"Name?" the guard interrupted, his fingers poised over the outdated computer's keyboard.

Jake was confused. "My name or his name?" he asked. He was entirely out of his element.

The guard looked up, his lips curling in slight amusement. "His name. I have to look him up in the system to see which block he's in."

"Oh…his name's Gregory Carver." As the man entered the information into his computer, Jake looked at his name tag. It read Officer Dabiew.

"Carver is in cell block A which means he can receive visitors at one o'clock." He clicked the mouse again. "Mmmmm...that's interesting," Officer Dabiew muttered. "Carver has never had a single visitor outside legal counsel." He looked at Jake. "What's your relation to him?" he asked curiously.

Instantly, Jake's cheeks flushed. He was surprised to feel such embarrassment at the question. His father was a cold-blooded murderer, the kind of dirt-bag Officer Dabiew dealt with on a daily basis. Shame washed over Jake; he felt his face grow hot. He stared at his boots and muttered, "He's my father."

The officer's eyes softened. He studied the boy standing before him who clearly wasn't like the usual characters who showed up every Saturday. A life of misery was not yet etched on his face. Curious now, he asked, "What made you decide to finally come here?"

As Jake quickly recounted his story, the officer's demeanor changed drastically. No longer was he aloof; he was definitely intrigued. This boy's courage impressed him, but he was also worried about the boy. He didn't feel good about this visit. This young man standing before him longed for a logical explanation for an extremely illogical act of violence. "Are you sure you don't want to come back with your grandparents?"

Jake shook his head. "I'm already here...I just want to get this over with."

"Ok then," Officer Dabiew consented, "we'll get started with the formalities. Do you have your driver's license with you?" he asked.

Jake pulled his wallet from his back pocket. His fingers trembled slightly as he pulled it out. He silently handed it over.

"Good. You wouldn't be able to visit without it, Jake." He turned away and scanned the identification in the copy machine. "Believe it or not, but your name is actually listed on your...um...Carver's visitors' list." He couldn't bring himself to say 'father.' He just couldn't equate the man from cell block A as this boy's father. "I see here that you're only seventeen," the guard said as he handed back Jake's license.

"Is that going to be a problem?" Jake asked uneasily.

"Not really. It just requires additional paperwork and a signature from the warden since you're a minor." He glanced at the clock on the wall. "It actually works out that you're so early. We should be able to get all of this done before one o'clock." He smiled at Jake as he passed him some forms to fill out.

*   *   *

Ryan looked in his rearview mirror and saw a long line of cars. He hadn't seen any vehicles with flashing lights in a few minutes. People were starting to become impatient. Ryan watched as three cars carefully performed u-turns. It was like watching an ungainly dance as the cars pirouetted away to find a detour. He turned to Adam who was obviously lost in thought, his head resting against the cool glass of the passenger door. Ryan was certain he was

194

thinking of Sandy. "What do you think is the shortest way to your house, Adam? I think it's time to turn this beast around and find a different way, don't you?"

"I hate sitting here," Adam replied. Suddenly, he gasped and jerked awkwardly as his cell phone vibrated in his pocket. "Oh, shit," he said grabbing his chest. "I thought I was being electrocuted." He fumbled in his pocket and pulled out his buzzing phone.

Ryan laughed. "You're an idiot, Adam. It's probably just Amber."

Adam gave him the finger and checked the number on the screen. It was his stepmother. "Hello?"

"Adam, it's Julia. Where are you?"

"There was an accident and we're stuck in traffic. We're about to turn around and take some back roads to get home. I should be there soon. Is Amber there?" he asked knowing that she most certainly was. Amber was never late for anything.

"I assume she's there. She was when I left anyway," Julia answered.

"What do you mean?" Adam asked anxiously. "You're not home? Is Dad home?" He could feel his heart begin to pound; he was afraid to hear Julia's response.

"No, he had to work and I'm at the mall. Don't worry—I called your brother to keep her company when I hit the detour. He's taking good care of her, I'm sure," she replied cheerfully.

Adam hung up the phone, his mouth agape. He turned to Ryan to explain, but Ryan was already attempting a three-point turn. He'd only heard half of the conversation, but he knew the danger awaiting Amber. Ryan's mind raced. He could probably be at Adam's house in five minutes. Would that be too late?

A strangled moan escaped from Adam's mouth. Vomit crawled from his roiling stomach as realization set in. He swallowed determinedly. All the puzzle pieces had fallen into place. He now knew the identity of Justin's angel, and he'd delivered her right to him.

*   *   *

Justin couldn't believe his luck. Here she was lying naked on his bed, her blond hair splayed upon his pillow. He admired her body. Tan lines from a summer of swimming and sunbathing showed faintly. He felt a stirring within him as his excitement mounted. There was one thing he had to do first. He took his camera from his desk and began taking pictures of Amber lying completely vulnerable. Each flash of the camera marked a stolen moment. He lay down beside her and snapped a close-up of the two of them, his lecherous smile, gleaming white, an utter perversity.

Justin set the camera on his dresser and aimed it at his bed. He turned the dial to the video function. He pulled off his shirt and locked his bedroom door. He strode back to his bed feeling invincible. He sat on the edge of his bed and grinned lasciviously at the camera.

196

CHAPTER 15

Getting the warden's permission was going to be much easier than Jake had initially anticipated. Since he was listed on his father's visitors' list and was coming from another state for just a one-time visit, Officer Dabiew said it was all really just a formality. By 10:30, Jake had finished his paperwork and was told to wait until it was processed and had all the necessary signatures. The contents of his pockets, including his wallet and cell phone, had been placed in one of the small metal lockers lining the wall behind the desk. He had also been summarily searched for contraband, which had consisted of a quick pat-down by Officer Dabiew and a trip through a metal detector. He now sat in a visitors' waiting room with four other people.

He glanced at the other visitors. They were all women. Three looked to be in their mid-twenties or thirties, and the other was older, maybe in her fifties. Jake had a while before one o'clock, so he studied the women surreptitiously under the guise of reading a magazine. The older female, a matronly black woman appeared to be engrossed in a James Patterson novel, but Jake knew her thoughts were elsewhere when he realized she hadn't turned a page in five minutes. He wondered if she were here visiting her son. He looked at the gray hair sprinkled around her temples and wondered what hardships had put them there.

The younger women mostly stared down into their laps. Occasionally, their attention would be drawn to the small colored television in the corner where a Lifetime movie played. They wore masks of complacency, but their haggard appearances told a different story. Even though they were young, Jake could see a lifetime of horrible experiences etched onto their faces.

He studied the blond in the corner. Even though Jake knew she'd attempted to dress nicely, he could tell the clothes were old and cheap, probably rescued from a Salvation Army thrift store. Her skirt and short-sleeved blouse did not match the cold weather. Her hair was obviously dyed, at least two inches of dark brown roots showing. She was restless, constantly smoothing down her frizzy hair or tapping her knee with a nicotine-stained finger. Jake surmised that she was here to see her boyfriend.

The woman who sat directly across from Jake wore tattered jeans and a low-cut sweater. Her fingernails were painted neon green and she had no fewer than six facial piercings. Her black hair had blue streaks running through it. She spent most of her time staring at her hands or looking absently at the wall above Jake's head.

The last woman sat to the right of Jake, wedged between the wall and the small bookshelf that held some magazines and a few tattered paperbacks. She was probably in her mid-thirties and appeared completely exhausted. Life had obviously sent her through the wringer, and she'd accepted it with quiet resignation. Occasionally, her eyes would close and Jake wondered if she were imagining a different life than the one she had been dealt.

Had it not been for the television, Jake would have been suffocated by the silence. No one spoke. No one made eye contact.

No one wanted to admit to the atrocities that had brought them all together that morning. As he looked at the women surrounding him, Jake was glad his grandparents had saved themselves and him from this emotionally taxing experience. His anger at them was still with him, a hard knot in his chest, but it had begun to loosen as he observed these women. Jake folded up his coat and placed it against the wall behind his neck. He would try to rest, but he didn't think the army of butterflies in his stomach would allow him to sleep.

*   *   *

Adam threw open the passenger door before Ryan had even come to a complete stop. He sprinted toward the front door and was in the house before Ryan could unfasten his seatbelt.

"Amber!" Adam shouted as he ran through the living room and up the stairs. The TV was still on, canned laughter echoing around the empty room. He took the steps two at a time and ran to Justin's bedroom door. He turned the knob, only to find it locked. He pounded on the door with his fists and shouted, "Justin, open this door now." He was absolutely frantic with fear and foreboding. *Oh, God, please don't let Amber be in there,* he begged.

Ryan joined him at that second. He pushed Adam aside and kicked at the doorknob. Pain rocketed up his shin and into his knee, but adrenalin surged through him. It took three more good kicks before the door finally splintered. The two boys worked together to shoulder it open, and the door finally slammed against the opposite wall.

Adam started into the room and froze. Justin was zipping up his jeans, and Amber was lying naked on his bed. "You son of a bitch!" Adam screamed, tears of helplessness blurring his vision. He swung his fists wildly at Justin, but most of them landed harmlessly.

"What the fuck are you doing here?" Justin yelled back. He easily caught Adam's flailing arms. "You're going to be sorry now!" he fumed, spittle flying into Adam's face. Justin let go of Adam and pulled back his fist, ready to teach his brother a lesson.

Ryan grabbed Justin's arm, spun him around, and punched him in the face. Blood spurted from his nose and ran freely over his lips. "What now, pussy? You're not so tough now, are you?" Ryan screamed into Justin's face. Blinded by fury, Ryan seized Justin's wrist and pulled him close once again, intent on beating him mercilessly.

Justin brought up his knee swiftly into Ryan's groin. Ryan's grip immediately loosened and Justin shook him off. As Ryan slumped onto his knees, holding his testicles, Justin kicked him in the chest. Ryan crashed into the dresser.

That's when Adam threw himself on Justin's back, shouting a string of unintelligible words. He managed to get his arm under Justin's chin and squeezed his forearm against his throat. He was not shocked to realize that he wanted to kill his brother. His rage was limitless.

Justin, staggering across the room, spun around and smashed his brother's back against the wall. Adam's head crashed into the drywall and a crater appeared. Justin felt the grip around his neck loosen and gasped for breath. He wasn't the least bit afraid. In fact, he was intoxicated with resentment and focused only on hurting Adam—the nuisance who had ruined his chance. Adam's back and head collided with the wall three more times before he slid off Justin's back and collapsed to the floor.

Ryan stood painfully and watched helplessly as Justin disappeared out the door. He could hear his footsteps running down the stairs. Ryan knelt beside Adam's prostrate form. "Adam, are you okay?"

Adam groaned in response and tried to sit up, but his head swam and his vision blurred. He closed his eyes. "Check on Amber," he slurred.

Ryan stood shakily and stepped toward the bed. He quickly shed his jacket and used it to cover Amber's naked body. "Amber, can you hear me?" he asked as he gently patted her cheek. He received no response, but he could hear her raspy breathing and see the flutter of her pulse in her neck. He reached into his pocket for his phone, dialed 911, and strode to the window just in time to see Justin speed down the driveway. The red Jeep Cherokee turned left onto the highway. Hot white anger flowed through Ryan's entire body. It took him a moment to even realize the operator was speaking to him. He quickly relayed what had happened and sat to wait for the police and ambulance. He checked on Adam once more before he sat beside Amber on the bed to hold her limp hand.

*   *   *

Ryan sat in the hospital waiting room with his parents, Jim and Kathy. His father paced the floor uneasily while his mother sat beside him rubbing his back. Normally, Ryan would have shrugged off any such public display of affection, but after the morning he'd had, he welcomed her comfort. He would never tell her this, though.

He was completely exhausted now, both physically and emotionally. He'd already spent an hour with two police officers and his parents in an empty hospital room telling them everything he knew. Well--almost everything. While Adam was being loaded into the ambulance, he had made Ryan promise not to mention Sandy's name.

The police scribbled furiously while Ryan told them everything, starting with Justin's "contest" and ending with the morning's events. It had been difficult for him to keep his composure while he recounted how they'd found Amber, naked and unconscious, and the fight that had ensued.

His mother wept openly and couldn't stop touching him—on his face, his back, his hand, his arm. It was almost like she couldn't believe this was real. Ryan felt like the whole thing was a bad dream, but he knew it wasn't. His swollen genitals, still throbbing, reminded him continuously with a drum roll of pain he felt all the way up to his ears. His father, on the other hand, was furious. At one point, when Ryan told the police how Adam's father had simply flushed away the pills, he'd left the room for about five minutes, swinging the door open so hard that it crashed against the wall.

When the policemen finally escorted Ryan and his parents back to the waiting room, they assured him that an APB had been issued on Justin's vehicle and that police in three counties were on the lookout. "Don't worry, Ryan, we'll find him," the one with dark hair told him before they left.

Now they sat—and waited—and his father marched back and forth. A very young nurse dressed in colorful scrubs approached them. She looked vaguely familiar to Ryan. She glanced around, making sure they were alone before she spoke. "I just saw the police leave, so I thought I'd give you an update. I'm really not supposed tell you about other patients, but I know you were there with Adam and Amber when…it happened. I think you deserve to know what's going on." She addressed Ryan, even though both of his parents now stood beside him. "Adam has a concussion and is being held for observation." She added softly, obviously embarrassed, "We can't reach his parents at the numbers you gave us. Do you have any other numbers we can try?"

"No, I took all the numbers for them from Adam's cell phone. He doesn't have any other relatives who live nearby either."

"Well, that just figures, doesn't it?" Jim sputtered angrily. "His one good son is in the hospital, and the bastard is probably at home flushing evidence."

Kathy put her hand on her husband's arm, hoping to calm him. He took a deep breath and nodded at his wife. She turned to the nurse. "What about Amber?" she asked.

"Amber's still unconscious. We're not sure how long the drug will last. It varies from person to person. She's had her stomach pumped and had some, um, tests."

Ryan looked away. He didn't want to imagine the kind of test the nurse was referring to. He'd seen enough *Law and Order SVU* to know about the rape kit. He was thankful that Amber had been unconscious.

"Are her parents with her?" Kathy asked the nurse.

"Yes, they got here awhile ago and have been sitting with her." She turned to Ryan. "They are very appreciative of you and Adam." She took Ryan's arm and led him away from his parents. "Actually, we all are. It's about time for that bastard to get caught."

Comprehension settled over Ryan like a cold, damp fog. He now remembered this girl. She was a year older and should have been graduating this year, but she'd dropped out of school last April. Her name was Kristen; they'd been in an art class together. Ryan's eyes found hers. "Did he rape you too?"

She shifted nervously from one foot to the other and spoke quickly, her words rushing together. "I never told anyone. It was so confusing. I didn't know what had happened. I just woke up and my clothes were all messed up. I just got out of there." Kristen exhaled deeply and met Ryan's eyes. "I've been weighed down by that secret for a long time now. That actually felt good to get off my chest."

"Are you going to report it to the police?" Ryan asked. He looked toward his parents over Kristen's head and found them staring back curiously.

Kristen gazed unwaveringly into Ryan's eyes and firmly replied, "You know what? I am. My shift ends in an hour, and I'm going directly to the police station. I've decided not to let Amber go through this alone."

"I know that Amber will appreciate that, and I suspect more girls will be coming forward real soon," Ryan said with confidence as he thought of Sandy.

*   *   *

Amber's parents had rushed to the hospital as soon as they received the phone call from the police. The officer had been very vague over the phone, telling them there had been an incident, that their daughter was unconscious but stable, and to come to Alice Hyde Hospital. Two policewomen and a nurse had met them in the lobby. They were led to a conference room where they were finally told of the drugging and sexual assault. Ironically, Patsy had been the strong one. Ben had broken down immediately, sobbing so hard that he'd begun to gasp for air. He was torn between wanting to kill Justin and needing to be with his daughter.

Patsy wanted answers, but none were forthcoming. Tests were being run, one of her rescuers was being questioned by the police, and the other boy was having a hard time concentrating enough to answer questions due to a concussion. They would have to wait.

Once Ben regained his composure, they were led directly to Amber's room where they immediately set up sentry, one on each side of her bed. She hadn't awakened yet. They sat beside her, each holding one of her hands, as their silent tears dropped on her blanket, the first teardrop quickly buried by others.

A soft tapping on the door interrupted their sorrow. Dr. Mackey's head appeared around the half-open door. "Mind if I come in?" he asked. He had two young daughters at home, so he couldn't imagine the torment this father was enduring. He entered in response to Patsy's nod. He pulled a chair closer to Ben's, pretending not to see him swiping hurriedly at the tears trailing down his face. "I'm Steve Mackey," he said shaking Ben's hand. He reached over the bed to shake Patsy's as well.

"When is she going to wake up?" Patsy asked anxiously.

"We can't say for certain. The boys who interrupted the assault are pretty certain the attacker used Rohypnol."

"The date rape drug?" Ben groaned miserably and turned back to his daughter. She looked so young. He smoothed her hair and caressed her cheek.

"The effects of Rohypnol can last up to eight hours, but I don't suspect she'll be asleep that long. We pumped her stomach fairly quickly—we think within forty minutes of her being drugged. We won't know definitively what she was given until tomorrow morning when the lab results come back, but we're pretty certain from the boy's description that that's what it was."

A heavy fog of silence descended upon the room, everyone avoiding the obvious question. Ben cleared his throat. "Was she…?" was all he managed to utter. He looked at the floor, unable to meet his wife's gaze. He stared at his hands as the doctor delivered the news.

*   *   *

Jake was led down a brightly lit hallway. The concrete block walls were painted a dingy gray, like socks washed too many times. The florescent lights hummed above his head.

The guard, a different one this time, pointed him to a hard plastic chair. "Carver should be out in a few minutes," he said dully before he turned and left.

Jake sank onto the chair. He was overcome by a tsunami of emotions and was suddenly exhausted. He looked around himself. The setup was just like every prison movie he'd ever seen and reminded him of the library's study carrels—except this was definitely not the library. To his left and right were wood dividers, creating a sense of privacy where none truly existed. Before him was a small ledge, almost like a desk but much more narrow with just enough room to prop one's elbows. An outdated, clunky phone hung on the wall to his right.

Other visitors were being led to seats nearby. The older woman from the waiting area was escorted past Jake. She walked erect with her head held high and kept her gaze straight, avoiding eye contact with the other visitors. Jake sat up a little straighter until the echo of slamming doors made him flinch. He folded in on himself once again. He wanted to leave—to run from this place and never look behind, but he couldn't. He needed to see him, and he needed to ask him why. Before long, Jake would have his answer. The window of Plexiglas before him would soon reveal his father's image. The orange chair on the other side would soon hold his father's body. Soon, the grimy, yellow phone would resonate with his father's voice.

Footsteps echoed against the hard floor. Jake's palms began to sweat, his stomach twisted, and his heart raced. He closed his eyes, afraid of what he would see. The steps stopped and a chair screeched across the floor. Jake's eyes flew open and locked onto the man now seated before him.

It was his father. Jake had expected to glimpse a mere shadow of the man he remembered, but there he sat—just as he appeared in every one of Jake's memories. The only difference was the thick, white scar that marked his neck. Greg smiled, picked up the phone, and motioned for Jake to do the same. Jake slowly complied.

"I'd recognize you anywhere, Jake," Greg said, overcome with emotion. Jake said nothing in return. Greg studied his son carefully; he was almost a man now, no longer the little boy who starred in his dreams. Jake reminded him of himself. He had his hair, his eyes, and his nose. "I think about you all the time, you know." He spoke quietly into the phone, attempting to put his son, who sat before him looking dazed, at ease.

All Jake could do was nod meekly as he shifted uncomfortably in his chair. Now that his father sat before him, he couldn't think of anything to say. All of his questions had disappeared, lodged somewhere between his brain and his mouth.

"Did your grandparents bring you?"

"No, I came alone," Jake croaked. He cleared his throat and stared at the scarring on his father's throat.

Greg noticed his gaze and lightly traced the puckered line. "I didn't cut deep enough," he muttered. "It's been a constant reminder." His voice filled with anguish as he met his son's eyes. "I should have been stronger—another couple millimeters would have done it." He could feel the prick of hot tears and blinked them back. He added bitterly, "I deserve this punishment. I deserve to be locked up like an animal." He repeatedly ran his palm over his cropped hair and looked down, afraid to read the resentment on his son's face.

Oddly enough, seeing Greg's weakness made Jake feel stronger. All of his tense muscles relaxed, and he loosened his vise-like grip on the phone. He watched his father stroke his head and realized that he felt no pity. Empowered now, Jake asked the question that had haunted him for so many years. "Why did you do it? What happened that morning?"

The knots of muscle along Greg's jaw line pulsed. He swung his head up slowly to meet his son's steely gaze. "I don't know," he stammered. "I hardly even remember anything."

"Were you fighting about something?" Jake prodded.

"Yes, but I can't remember what the fight was about. I was so angry all I saw was red." Greg spoke in a monotonous voice. His eyes looked through Jake, not at him. He continued as though in a trance. "The first memory I have is holding the knife. There was blood on it. It was hot and sticky. Then I saw Elizabeth...she was dead. I knew I had done it, but I couldn't remember doing it to her. It was like another part of me killed her. I thought there was a monster inside me, so I tried to kill it with the same knife when the police showed up."

"So you just snapped?" Jake's voice began to rise. This explanation was *not* the answer he sought. "Is that what you're telling me?"

It took a few seconds for Greg to focus back on Jake. His son's agony sent a torrent of emotions through him. "I don't know what you want me to say, Jake," he pleaded.

"I *need* for there to be a reason," Jake cried frantically. "You can't be a normal person one minute and a murderer the next. That doesn't make sense!" Jake suddenly felt sick. The room was too hot, and the air was pungent with sweat, mold, and desperation. Nearby voices created a buzz in his ears. He wanted to run away, but he was firmly rooted to his chair.

"I can't give you a reason. I just can't, Bug," Greg confessed.

Jake became deaf to all else. Only one word repeated itself in his brain—Bug. No one but his parents had called him that. "Goodnight, Bug." He heard his mother's voice as though she sat next to him. Hearing his nickname brought a whirlwind of memories storming through his mind. He became frozen—unable to move or speak. He could feel his heart beating, and he could feel his chest contracting and expanding. All life functions operated on autopilot as his brain dove recklessly into the past. Each memory played quickly like a home movie on fast forward, the images grainy and slightly out of focus. Jake saw everything as though his younger self were the one holding the camera.

He sat in the back seat of a car, cradled firmly by his car seat. He was alone, but the driver's side door was wide open. The red eye of the traffic light glowered at him. He looked to his left when he heard his father's voice. Greg was attempting to open another man's car door. He gesticulated wildly and banged on the window, his yells getting louder, more demanding, and his face was getting redder by the second. When the light turned green, the other car sped away, leaving Greg standing in the road. Cars honked impatiently.

"Daddy, why are you mad at that man?" a scared voice asked as Greg climbed inside the car.

"I'm not mad at him, Bug." He leaned back and tickled Jake's knee. "The man needed directions and he couldn't hear very well, so I had to yell. That's all," he said reassuringly. The ice cream cone five minutes later helped meld the moment in the car into an enjoyable afternoon.

SNAP! This time he saw a pair of boots sticking out from behind the azalea bush in the backyard. He moved forward to see his father kneeling before a freshly dug hole. "What are you doing, Daddy?" a childish voice asked curiously. His father spun around, surprised, and that's when Jake saw Mrs. Clark's dead Pomeranian in the hole. "What happened to Honey?"

Jake's father stood and turned the boy around and pointed him toward the house. "She got really sick and died, so I'm burying her for Mrs. Clark. She was too sad to do it herself."

SNAP! Another memory flashed before his eyes. His father was nowhere in sight this time. Jake was in the kitchen where his mother was killed. He remembered the gauzy yellow curtains that hung over the window. His mother walked in carrying a laundry basket. He heard a child's giggle. "Mommy, you look like a raccoon."

"Oh, do I?" she replied playfully as she kneeled before him. Two small fingers gently traced the black bruises under his mother's eyes. "Mommy was a klutz and smashed her nose against the closet door. Can you believe that, my little Bug?" She clucked him on the chin and disappeared into the next room.

He came back to the present with a jerk. A multitude of silent accusations built up in Jake's throat. He was mute, but his mind screamed. The memories had blasted through him like a current of electricity. Jake had never understood the significance of these events when they had occurred. He'd been too young to understand, and he'd forgotten them all—until now. In just a few seconds he realized that his father wasn't perfect. He hadn't just snapped. There had been signs; he just hadn't been old enough to comprehend them. The man who sat in front of him was an expert at hiding the monster within. That's why no one else had known anything was wrong and how his grand-parents had been duped.

"What's the matter? Cat got your tongue?" Greg asked stonily.

Jake looked up, startled. Had it only been two days ago when Amber had asked the same thing? He shook his head, unsuccessfully trying to rid himself of the images that had bombarded his mind.

212

Even though Jake wanted nothing better than to simply get up and put as many miles as possible between himself and his father, he still needed some answers. Jake dug his fingernails into his palms. "You killed Mrs. Clark's dog. You abused my mother before you killed her. Why?" he asked simply. He met his father's eyes and tried to appear calm, but his voice wavered, giving him away.

Greg looked down, breaking away from his son's steely gaze. He collapsed forward and held his head in his hands. He crumpled before Jake's eyes. A few moments passed. Jake gave his father time to compose himself and watched as his father's broad shoulders shook occasionally. He looked around uncomfortably, wondering how long he should wait before breaking his father's silence. One of the guards, who had been standing behind the prisoners, moved closer and eyed Greg suspiciously and without compassion.

Suddenly, Greg looked up, his eyes completely dry. He pulled his chair closer and leaned toward the glass partition, his nose almost touching it. His lips curled cruelly into a smile. "So, you do remember some things?"

Jake's stomach turned sour. Greg hadn't been crying; he'd been laughing. He stared into his father's amused eyes, and a lightning bolt of anger surged through him, electrifying his senses. He stood abruptly and knocked over his chair in the process. "You son of a bitch," he growled into the phone. The lone guard who monitored the visitors' side started toward Jake from down the hall. "What the hell is wrong with you?

You're a psychopath!" Jake was shouting now, and the guard hurried his way.

"Actually," Greg said wryly, bored now with his son's dramatics, "sociopath is the correct term."

"Is there a problem here?" The guard had now reached Jake's side. Meanwhile, three guards, with their nightsticks at the ready, had crept behind Greg.

Jake gasped for breath; nausea bubbled in his stomach. Every muscle was taut. He wanted to break through that plastic barrier and rip the smirk off his father's vile face. He couldn't speak, he couldn't move, and, worst of all, he couldn't slam down the phone to end the nightmare.

His father stood and leaned toward the partition. He pointed at Jake and said into the phone, "Just don't forget that there's a whole lot of me in you." Greg threw back his head in a fit of maniacal laughter.

Jake threw down the phone and watched as the guards threw Greg to the floor and quickly subdued him. He spun around and sprinted down the hall, ignoring the shouts that followed him.

Chapter 16

Ryan had almost fallen asleep, lulled by his mother's hand rubbing rhythmic circles on his back. He heard a door down the hall open and close and looked up to see Ben Green walking quickly toward him. He was a mess. His hair stuck up at odd angles, his shirt was only half tucked in, his eyes were red-rimmed, and tears rolled freely down his cheeks. Ryan stood and took two steps toward him, thinking the worst, but Ben wrapped Ryan in a huge bear hug that lifted him off the floor. When he was finally released, Ryan stood, dumfounded. "You got there in time." Ben's voice cracked as he grabbed Ryan's shoulders. "You got there in time."

It took a moment for Ryan to process what Mr. Green was telling him. When the realization sank in, a smile stretched across Ryan's face. Relief rushed through his entire body—he felt weak with it.

Kathy stood and hugged Ben to her. "Thank God. That's so good to hear," she gushed.

Ben turned back to Ryan. "We can never thank you and Adam enough. If you had arrived a few minutes later…" an anguished sob escaped, and he couldn't bring himself to finish the sentence.

Jim clapped Ben on the back and said softly, "I can't even imagine what you're feeling."

Ben's jaw tightened. "I want to kill the little bastard; that's how I'm feeling." He heard the venom in his own voice and was startled by it. He looked back at Ryan, and his voice softened. "I'm just so glad you stopped him. You will never understand how grateful I feel." He hugged Ryan to him again. "Thank you," he whispered in his ear.

Ben abruptly turned, overcome with emotion, walked back down the hall and slipped into Amber's room.

Thirty minutes later, Kristen returned. She tapped Ryan on the shoulder, and he jumped at her touch. He'd fallen into a deep sleep as soon as Ben Green had given him the good news. "Sorry. I didn't mean to scare you," she said sheepishly. "The doctor said it's okay to see Adam now."

Ryan looked at his parents. "I'm fine. You guys don't have to stay here, you know. I'll visit Adam for a little while and wait for Jake. He has to turn up at some point, and I feel like I should be the one to explain what happened to Amber."

"You're a good friend, Ryan." Kathy caressed her son's cheek. She glanced over at her husband and stated bluntly, "I don't know about you, but I'm going to stay here and wait." She nodded toward her son. "He's not leaving my sight."

"I'll wait too. I'm still too riled up to go home. How about I get us some sandwiches from the deli down the street?" Kathy handed the car keys to him. Before   he left, he put an arm around his son. "I'm really proud of you and Adam. Be sure to tell him that for me, would you?"

"Sure, Dad...don't get all Hallmark moment on me here. I don't think I can take any more tears right now," he said jokingly, but his voice cracked with emotion.

216

Jim gave his son a few reassuring thumps on his back and turned toward the elevator. He could feel tears stinging his eyes but turned before his son could see them.

"See you in a bit, dad," Ryan called after his father's retreating form.

The gravity of his son's situation was beginning to overwhelm him. Jim was glad the elevator was empty. He took a few gulping breaths to steady his nerves. Ryan could be the one lying in the hospital bed right now. He hated to even consider the more extreme alternative, but as the door slid open and revealed the bustling lobby, Jim couldn't help but feel pleased at Ryan's quick thinking and heroic actions.

Ryan gave a little wave to his mother and followed the nurse to room 212. When Ryan entered the room, he expected to see the worst--Adam attached to a bunch of machines and a roll of white gauze wrapped around his head, but he just sat there, looking fairly normal.

"Okay, guys, you can only visit for a few minutes," Kristen announced. "I'll come and get you when your time is up," she said to Ryan before she left the room.

"How're you feeling, chief?" Ryan asked.

"My head is killing me," Adam replied slowly and very quietly. "I just want to sleep, but they won't let me. And, they won't tell me anything either."

Ryan sat on the edge of the bed. "Luckily I'm here to fill you in," he said, keeping his tone light. "I'll tell you the best news first. Amber was not raped."

Adam smiled broadly. He looked much less miserable all of the sudden. "We got there in time?" he asked incredulously.

"Yes, and everyone is extremely thankful. Amber's dad thinks we're heroes, and my dad wanted me to tell you how proud he is."

Adam let the good news sink in for a few moments. Slowly, he turned his face away from Ryan and gazed out the window. "Has my dad shown up?"

"No. They've left a bunch of messages for him, but..."

"I don't know why I expected him to come," Adam interrupted. Tears slid across his cheeks and dropped onto the pillowcase. "He doesn't care about me," he murmured despondently.

Ryan didn't know how to comfort his friend. He couldn't make excuses for

Adam's father. He awkwardly patted Adam's foot and listened helplessly to his friend's gut-wrenching sobs.

*   *   *

All of Jake's pent up anger and frustrations finally found vent once he reached his truck in the parking lot. He'd barely held it together while he gathered his possessions at the front desk. Officer Dabiew must have sensed Jake's distress; he hadn't asked a single question about the visit and had quickly handed over Jake's things. Once the door of the prison swung shut behind him, a torrent of tears streamed down his face. Once inside the privacy of his truck, he cried for his mother--at the helplessness she must have felt in the stranglehold of her marriage. He wept for his grandparents and himself and for the futures that had been stolen away from them by one depraved individual. His emotions shifted between sorrow, hatred, rage, and self-pity. He pounded on the steering wheel until his palms ached.

It was almost two before the crushing weight on Jake's chest eased slightly. His eyes, dry now, were swollen, red, and raw. All of the windows in the truck were fogged up, obliterating his view of the prison. As the defroster finally began to exhale warm air onto the glass, Jake checked his phone. He had 37 missed calls and several voicemail messages. Guilt crept over Jake as he listened to the worry in Nana's voice. There were three messages from Amber. In the first, she was definitely concerned about his discovery of the news article. In the second, annoyance edged her voice, and in the third, she was clearly angry at his thoughtlessness and demanded that he call her immediately. As Jake deleted each message, he hoped that everyone would be forgiving and realize that this was something he'd had to do. Now, he realized just how foolish he'd been. If he'd only just awakened his grandparents, perhaps he could have avoided this nightmare he'd created for himself.

The next message was from Ryan, and it made the tiny hairs on Jake's neck and arms stand on end. "Hey, Jake, you need to call me back when you get this. Amber was in an accident and is in the hospital. She's not badly injured, but she has to stay overnight for observation. We just got here, so I'll call with an update when I hear more."

219

Jake shifted into reverse as Ryan's voice again came over the phone. "We're still at the hospital. Amber's parents are with her. I plan on waiting around here for you, so call me. Don't do anything crazy getting here. She's going to be fine, and she's sleeping so it's not like you can talk to her anyway."

Jake maneuvered the truck over two speed bumps before he could dial Ryan's number. "Where have you been?" Ryan chastised by way of a greeting. "Your grandparents have been going crazy." Jake heard some muffled voices and immediately recognized Nana in the background asking to speak to him. Jake could hear the phone being shuffled about.

"Where are you, Jake?" Nana asked. Fear and dread cloaked every word.

"I saw him," Jake whispered. He cleared his throat, determined not to cry. "It was horrible, Nana," he croaked. There was only silence at the other end of the phone. Was she mad? Disappointed? Betrayed?

Nana had a suspicion that Jake had driven to the prison, but she just couldn't believe that he'd actually done it. What had he said to the man who'd murdered Elizabeth? She finally found her voice. "Oh, honey, I wish you'd waited. We could have gone with you. You didn't have to do that all on your own."

"I know, but I was so angry and confused, and I just left without even knowing what I was going to do." Jake braked at a stop sign. He rested his head on the steering wheel but only for a second. He had a new worry now--Amber. He had to file away his visit to the prison for now. "I'm leaving now. I can be at the hospital in two and a half hours. Is Amber really all right? What happened?"

"Yes, she's fine. She's still sleeping," Nana replied, purposely avoiding Jake's other question. She'd been shocked when Ryan called to tell her about Justin's attack on Amber. She wasn't about to tell Jake the truth when he had yet to drive so far. She was glad that Ryan had had the sense not to tell the truth when he left his previous messages. She hurriedly ended the conversation before he could ask about any details. "You shouldn't be talking and driving, so I'll see you soon. Drive carefully." She handed the phone back to Ryan.

"It sounds like we have a lot to talk about, buddy. We'll be here waiting. Hopefully, Amber will be awake by the time you get here," Ryan said reassuringly.

"You know what, Ryan? I think that's the first time you've ever called her by her actual name. Are you not telling me something?" Jake asked, suspicious now of Ryan's uncharacteristic compassion.

"Jake, Nana is standing right next to me. I don't really feel like getting smacked for using one of Amber's awesome nicknames." Ryan managed to laugh before hanging up.

*   *   *

When Jake finally pulled into the hospital's parking lot, a light dusting of snow had begun to fall again. Luckily, he'd had good weather; the roads had stayed clear and he'd made good time. As the old pickup truck shuddered to a stop, Jake shouldered open his door, which groaned begrudgingly, and jogged to the front doors. He approached a gray haired woman at the information counter. "I'm here to see Amber Green. Can you tell me which room she's in?" he asked. Jake nervously tapped the reception desk as the woman slowly typed Amber's name into the computer.

The pinging of the elevator drew Jake's attention. Ryan stepped out but held his arm between the two doors to keep them open. Jake looked at him gratefully.

"It's like I'm psychic," Ryan quipped in amazement. He motioned for Jake to join him in the elevator.

"Never mind," Jake said to the still-typing woman as he hurried to the elevator.

Ryan punched the button for the second floor as soon as Jake got inside. "I've been watching out the window and saw your hunk 'o junk pull in," he explained.

"How's Amber? Is she awake yet?" Jake asked anxiously. The elevator seemed to hang in space, creeping upward slowly millimeter by millimeter.

"Not yet," Ryan answered.

"Why not? What's the matter? Why has she been unconscious so long?" Jake's questions echoed unanswered in the confines of the elevator.

Ryan surreptitiously studied his friend's reflection in the metal of the elevator doors. He was a different person. His clothes and hair were disheveled, but the main difference was in his eyes. They were glazed over. They were exhausted. They were desperate. "Listen, I'll tell you everything after you've seen her. We'll take a walk and…"

"You'll tell me now," Jake growled menacingly. "I'm not waiting another second."

The elevator doors opened. Jake strode out, but Ryan grabbed his elbow and pulled him into the empty room where the police had questioned him earlier. He shut the door and leaned against it. "I *will* tell you everything, but you have to promise me one thing first."

"What's that?" Jake interjected angrily. His heart beat hollowly in his heaving chest. He was afraid to hear what Ryan had to say about Amber.

Ryan pointed to a chair. He spoke forcefully. "You have to sit in that chair the entire time. You will *not* get up until I'm done. You have to realize that you're in a hospital, and you can't go around acting like a lunatic. You'll scare people."

Jake sat, anxious now. Something bad had happened. He knew it wasn't just 'an accident.' "I promise to sit here. Just tell me what happened."

Ryan told Jake everything he'd told the police several hours before. Jake's reaction to Amber's attack had been unanticipated. Ryan had expected him to become enraged, but, instead, Jake wept openly, holding his head in his hands. His day had been fraught with devastation, and the only emotion he could summon at the moment was sorrow. Anger would come eventually, unbending and relentless, but, for now, tears were his only companion.

Ryan, uncomfortable with Jake's outburst, fetched Nana to comfort Jake. The two stayed in the room until Papa interrupted them ten minutes later to tell them Amber had awakened and was asking for Jake. Before entering Amber's room, Jake splashed cold water on his face in the restroom. He needed to be strong for her. He took a few deep breaths before walking steadily into her room.

"Jake," Ben Green said, taking his hand and shaking it, "we're glad you're here. Amber's been worried about you."

Patsy waved at Jake and kissed Amber on the cheek. "We'll be back in a few minutes after we talk to the doctor about getting you discharged." She motioned to her husband. "Come on, Ben, let's give these two some privacy."

Jake sat on the edge of Amber's bed. He carefully smoothed her hair away from her face. He could tell she was a little groggy and not entirely herself, but she was awake. She was safe. She was whole. "Ryan told me everything. I'm sorry I wasn't there to protect you." He kissed her forehead. He added softly, "And I'm sorry I ran off without calling. If I'd just called you, you wouldn't have been at Adam's house this morning. None of this would have happened."

Amber struggled to sit up. "Don't be an idiot," she sputtered. "You can't

possibly think *you're* to blame here. Did you cause the car accident that made Adam and Ryan late? Did you tell Adam's father to go to the office and Julia to meet one of her boyfriends?" Her voice grew shriller as she continued. "Did you tell Justin to drug my orange juice?" She lay back heavily onto her pillows once again, fighting for composure, but tears rolled down Amber's cheeks. Jake wiped them away with his thumb and handed her a tissue. He carefully laid down beside her on the narrow bed; neither spoke.

224

Jake wrapped his arm protectively around Amber. They each fought inwardly to regain a foothold in normalcy, but they were both too broken, and silence was the glue holding them barely together.

Ten minutes later, when Patsy returned, she found Jake lying beside Amber. He was sound asleep. Amber put her finger over her lips. Patsy sat in the chair beside the bed. "They still want to keep you overnight," she whispered.

Amber nodded, clearly disappointed.

"Doctor Mackey said you could be released first thing in the morning, though. We'll stay with you until visiting hours are over at seven. Your father went to get your sisters, so they could see you with their own eyes. They've been worried sick."

Jake stirred and slowly opened his eyes. He sat up quickly when he noticed Patsy sitting beside the bed.

"Jake, you should go home and get some sleep. You look wiped out, and Amber has to stay overnight."

Jake nodded and stood up. "I'll come visit you tomorrow, Amber." He blew her a kiss. "Bye, Mrs. Green."

Patsy stood up to give Jake a quick hug. "Why don't you come over for brunch at eleven tomorrow morning? Amber will be out of this place by then, and we'll have some chocolate chip pancakes."

"That sounds good. I'll see you both tomorrow then." Jake waved over his shoulder as he left the room. He shut the door quietly behind himself.

Nana and Papa both stood when he returned to the waiting area. "How is she?" Nana asked wringing her hands with worry.

"As far as her health, she'll be okay, but she has to spend the night here so the nurses can watch her." Jake shoved his hands into the pockets of his jeans. "She's really angry, though, not that I can blame her," he added as guilt washed over him once again. He felt so selfish. He had run away like a child and left everyone else to worry. Jake allowed himself to be wrapped up in comfort when Nana hugged him tightly.

He felt Papa's hand rest soothingly on his head. "Maybe you should check on Adam before we take you home. He's in room 212." He nodded in the direction of Adam's room.

Jake took a moment to gather himself before visiting Adam. He opened the door a crack and peeked inside. Ryan was sitting in a chair next to Adam's bed. ESPN was playing quietly on the TV, but neither of the boys was paying much attention to the show. Jake stood awkwardly at the foot of the bed. "How are you feeling, Adam?"

It was like a dam had burst. All of Adam's pent up frustrations came rushing out. "Like everything's all my fault," Adam exploded. "I should have gone to the police a long time ago. Now look what happened. You must hate me."

"What are you talking about, Adam?" Jake asked almost angrily. "You and Ryan saved her. He would have raped her, but you stopped him." Jake sat down at the end of the bed and patted Adam's foot reassuringly. "I think we're all ready to blame ourselves. Justin's probably the only one who doesn't feel guilty," Jake added spitefully.

Adam choked on the next words. "My brother is a monster. Do you know how that feels?" he asked frustrated.

"Yes, I know exactly how you feel." He shifted uncomfortably on the bed. He hadn't meant to say that. He looked at his friends; questioning faces looked back. It was time to tell them the truth. He took a deep breath and started with that morning's fateful quest. When he finished telling them about the day's visit, a burden was lifted. His secret, his veiled adversary, was finally crushed. He felt closer to his friends than ever before. He'd never known it, but he and Adam shared a hidden fear—that the evil in their families was somehow ingrained in them. Before he left, he gave Adam a quick hug. "You are *not* your brother," Jake declared loudly and with conviction, "and I am *not* my father."

Jake left the hospital with his grandparents, and, thankfully, Papa drove his truck home. Exhaustion weighed heavily upon him, and he still had to explain his visit to the prison to his grandparents. The hot air from the heater and the soft music playing from the radio lulled him. His eyelids drooped as he succumbed to the peace that only sleep would bring.

Chapter 17

Jake slept soundly until the slam of a car door woke him. He rolled over and glanced at his clock. It was nine. He felt guilty for leaving the morning chores to his grandfather once again, but the warmth of his bed was too appealing, and he did not want to budge. He heard a knock on the door and Nana greeting Ryan warmly. Jake rolled out of his comfortable bed and threw on some clean clothes. The stairs creaked with each of Ryan's steps. "Come on in," Jake called out before Ryan even had a chance to knock.

"How did you know I was there?" he asked in amazement.

"The stairs give you away every time," Jake answered logically. "What's up?" Ryan was known for sleeping in until noon on the weekends. Jake could only think of one thing that would bring him to his house this early in the morning. "Did they find Justin?" he asked full of excitement.

Ryan started fidgeting with the pens on Jake's desk. "Um, no." He couldn't bring himself to look at Jake. He flipped through a paperback on the nightstand.

"Okay, then why are you here so early?" Jake reached over and took the novel out of Ryan's hands. He tossed it onto his unmade bed.

Ryan was nervous to verbalize his plan. The idea had sounded good this morning when he lay awake, unable to sleep because of his racing mind, but now it just seemed stupid. "Well," he started slowly, "I was thinking that *we* should look for him." He hurried on before Jake could interrupt. "We know a lot of 'out of the way' places where Justin likes to party." He looked at Jake who was staring out the window and was sorry that he'd come over. He shrugged his shoulders almost apologetically. "I was just thinking that we could probably find him before the police."

Raw energy crackled through Jake's body. Even his fingertips tingled. "Yeah, let's do it." He smiled at Ryan. He actually felt good about something.

"Really?" Ryan asked incredulously. "I thought you'd think it was a stupid idea."

"No, I think it's a great idea. Amber and Adam aren't going to feel safe until he's caught, and, you're right--we know this area like the backs of our hands." Jake was getting excited. "If we see his Jeep, we'll call the police." He slapped Ryan's back and pulled on his socks. "We just need an excuse to tell Nana. She won't let me out of the house if she knows what we're up to."

"We could tell her that I need your help moving all of my mom's junk out of the spare bedroom since Adam's going to be staying at my house," Ryan suggested.

"Nice one," Jake praised. "That'll work on Amber's parents too. I'm supposed to go to their house at eleven for brunch, but we won't be back in time."

"Okay, I'll wait downstairs while you call them." Ryan rubbed his hands together excitedly. "We're like detectives. I'll be Starsky and you'll be Hutch," he called out as he sailed down the stairs.

"You're an idiot," Jake called after him. He dialed the Green's phone number and spoke to Mrs. Green. He felt bad lying to her, but more pressing matters needed to be dealt with.

*　　　*　　　*

"Do you have any other ideas?" Jake asked. They'd driven to all the typical high school party spots--Split Rock, the John Hill Road turnoff, the CC campground and the pinnacle. Giant snowflakes floated sleepily onto the windshield of Ryan's car.

"We could try the gorge," Ryan suggested. He flipped on the wipers and cleared the snow off the glass.

"We might as well. It's not that far away." Jake shrugged. "We'll call it a day after we check it out." The positive attitude he'd had a couple of hours ago was being replaced by something else…something sordid. As the boys neared Burke, the rage Jake had set aside yesterday was beginning to bubble up inside, a relentless slow boil. He bit his thumbnail and stared out the window. He silently willed Ryan to drive faster. He was filled with an unsettling uncertainty. Justin needed to be found one way or another because Amber and Adam deserved some peace.

Ryan turned right onto the dirt road. Neither of the boys said a word as the car bounced over potholes. This was their last possibility. As they reached the end of a row of tall pine trees, the parking lot came into view. It was empty, and Jake's stomach fell with disappointment. "Shit," he yelled and slammed his fist against the dashboard.

"I really thought he'd be here," Ryan said, exasperated. He put the car in park. "Think! There has to be another place. Maybe we should call Adam," he suggested as he took out his phone.

"Look!" Jake shouted excitedly. "Are those tire tracks?"

Ryan looked to where Jake was pointing off to the right. Sure enough, there they were, almost completely obliterated by the falling snow. "Good eyes," Ryan exclaimed happily. "Where do you think he parked? I don't see his car."

"We could just follow the tracks," Jake pointed out. "He's probably behind those rocks. He does have four wheel drive." Jake felt the blood coursing through his veins. It had to be Justin. Who else would be hiding here? The slow boil increased steadily, but he tried to appear calm. He craved justice, and now it was at hand.

Ryan picked up his phone. "Do you want to call the police or should I?" "Whoa…wait," Jake said hurriedly. "We're not even one hundred percent sure that it's him. We need to see his Jeep. Then we can call for backup." Jake opened the car door. "I'll sneak over there. If I see Justin's car, I'll give you a thumbs up."

Ryan looked at Jake nervously. "I don't think that's a good idea. He's dangerous, Jake. He took out Adam and me." He looked Jake up and down. "I'm pretty sure he can beat your scrawny ass with one arm."

"I'm not going to confront him," Jake reassured his friend. "I'm just going to see if it's him. I'm not going to mess with that psycho." Jake swung his legs out of the car and stood, pulling on his gloves. Before he shut the door, he leaned back in and said, "I'll be back in a few minutes. Look for the signal."

Ryan watched him walk away. The parking lot ended before the massive pile of rocks. A chain normally blocked any cars from driving beyond. Ryan was too far away to see if the chain was still in place, but he knew it certainly wouldn't be too difficult to remove it. The mound of boulders was a good hiding spot, especially with the snow erasing any signs of his Jeep's tire tracks. Ryan fiddled with the radio. He couldn't care less about listening to music, but it kept him distracted. When he glanced up, Jake was nowhere in sight. "Oh, shit," he exclaimed, climbing quickly out of the car.

*   *   *

Justin's red Jeep glared obscenely against the snowy backdrop. Its engine had recently been turned off. As it cooled, its rhythmic ticking interrupted the cold calm. Jake edged around the pile of rocks. He could see that the driver's seat had been reclined, but he wasn't close enough to see if Justin was laying there. The crunching of his boots sounded like thunder as he warily approached the vehicle. Just then, a flash of green caught his eye. He swung his head to the left and could just make out a person weaving among the trees. If everything hadn't been covered in a blanket of snow, Jake would never have seen him.

The trees, stripped now of their leaves, didn't provide much cover. A few pine trees, sprinkled here and there, momentarily hid Justin, but Jake's view was mostly unobstructed as he zeroed in on him moving toward the top of the waterfall. He knew that Justin hadn't seen him by the way he casually meandered up the incline. Jake, reacting on instinct, quickly followed the path that would bring him vengeance, glad to have the element of surprise on his side.

Jake's heartbeat kept time with his quickening footsteps. He was almost to the top. Naked branches grabbed at his jacket and tugged on his jeans, but he didn't waver. He continued on relentlessly, not the least bit tired. Instead, he felt invincible, ready to defeat his demons. All other thoughts vanished from Jake's mind as he continued steadily upward. He pushed away thoughts of Ryan who was, without a doubt, chasing after him by now. He forgot about his father's evil smirk and cutting words, and he even forgot, in that infinitesimal drop of time, about the seed of hate that had blossomed within him. Only an image of Amber remained--her contagious smile, her bright eyes, her golden hair reflecting the sun. He was blinded by this vision, and that's why, once he'd cleared the forest and stumbled into the clearing at the top of the falls, he didn't notice the branch come swinging toward his head. THWACK!

Jake found himself on the snow-covered ground. His head pounded and his eyes blurred. He blinked furiously in an attempt to clear his vision. He was staring at two black sneakers. Drops of blood stained the pristine snow. It took a moment for Jake to realize it was his blood; he could feel rivulets of it running down his scalp. It was almost soothing, like when Amber ran her fingers through his hair.

"What's your plan now, Jake?" Justin asked in a sinister voice. He knelt down so Jake could see him, but he made sure not to get too close. He looked around but didn't see anyone else approaching. Had Jake really come by himself? "Where are the cops? Or were you planning on taking care of me yourself?"

Justin's voice reached through the suffocating fog in Jake's brain, causing a flood of anger to surge through his entire body. There was a roaring in his ears that Jake soon realized was the sound of rushing water. They were at the top of the gorge near the waterfall. Everything fell back into place as Jake's mind cleared. His head still pounded painfully, and fingers of blood still oozed from the cut on his head, but Jake's heart raced with sudden clarity.

*   *   *

Ryan had started after Jake immediately. Once he'd reached Justin's Jeep and found it empty, he'd grabbed for his cell phone to call the police. Unfortunately, he'd left it in his car, so he'd sprinted back to make a very frantic call. The dispatcher had assured him an officer would be there within ten minutes, but Ryan hadn't waited. The police could follow their footprints, he'd reasoned.

Ryan had never noticed the steepness of the trail before, but, then again, he'd never run up it. His sneakers slid on the snow, and he grabbed onto a tree branch to keep from falling. He cursed himself for putting on his Nikes that morning, but he hadn't anticipated ever leaving the car. His strategy all along had been to simply search for Justin's car. He hadn't planned on running through the woods to save his friend from a maniac. His breathing was ragged, more from fear than fatigue, and puffs of frozen air rushed from his open mouth. When Ryan burst into the clearing, he skidded to a stop. What he saw chilled him to the bone. Jake and Justin were about fifty yards away, fighting dangerously close to the rim of the waterfall.

*　　*　　*

Jake wanted to kill Justin. He had never been so sure of anything in his whole life. This realization should have scared him, but it gave him assurance instead. This… this…thing standing before him was a monster. How many lives had he ruined? He deserved to die. Jake stood shakily, but with each passing second, he felt his strength grow. He wiped the blood from his face with his gloved hand.

"What's the matter, Jake? Are you sorry I had a little taste of your girlfriend?" he taunted as he licked his lips. As Jake walked toward him, Justin moved backward, toward the mouth of the gorge. "She has a hot little body, that's for sure," he added cruelly. Justin had nothing to lose now. The hate he felt for Adam and Ryan could just as well be used against Jake. He felt an overwhelming urge to destroy someone, and he wasn't particular about who it would be. "I do have some pictures that I'm sure you'd love to see."

Jake rushed toward him and tackled him to the ground. He kneeled on Justin's chest and pummeled his face fiercely. His brain was not working correctly; he was an animal, primal and savage, growling as he continued to flail wildly.

Justin bucked him off, rolled away, and stood on shaky legs. He was dazed by Jake's violence. This was not what he'd expected. Justin took stock of his injuries. His left eye was half closed, his eyebrow was bleeding, and his mouth was filled with blood. Some of his teeth were missing, and he wondered absently if he'd swallowed them. He felt dizzy and swayed slightly as he stared at a hazy Jake.

Jake looked at his hands. His gray gloves were now bright red with blood. How much of it was his own? He heard a police siren in the distance. He took a step toward Justin. Then another.

Justin stepped back as Jake approached, edging even closer to the mouth of the gorge. He put up his hands in surrender as the shrieking of the siren became louder. It was all over now.

"Justin!" Jake screamed. "Stop!"

Justin barely had time to register what was happening before gravity failed him. His left foot slipped over the edge and he fell forward, scrambling for a foothold, a handhold, anything. His elbows stopped him for a moment, but his chin crashed against the unforgiving rock and he slipped further. His fingers clawed at smooth rock while his feet thrashed at the side of the cliff.

Jake dove for the edge and grabbed Justin's arm. It slowed his descent enough for his right foot to find a small rock protrusion. He could barely feel it under his toes. Would it be enough?

Droplets of sweat appeared on Jake's brow. As long as Justin's foot stayed on that rock, he could hold him. He could hear a distant voice shouting, and he knew it was Ryan. If he could hold on until Ryan got there, Justin would be safe. Suddenly, the chunk of rock disintegrated under Justin's foot, and Jake could feel the heavy pull as Justin's full weight hung on his arms. His shoulders screamed. He could feel himself being dragged toward the edge and attempted to dig the toe of his boots into the ground, but the snow was too slippery.

"Don't let me go," Justin begged, panic evident in his voice. Desperation clouded his eyes.

"Help is almost here. Hang on." He could hear Ryan shouting, closer now.

Jake stared into the black of Justin's eyes, and even as his muscles strained against the pull of Justin's body, his hand trembled with knowing. This would be his very last…wavering.

CHAPTER 18

A few warm days in the fifties had finally melted the four inches of snow. The birds weren't sure what they were supposed to do. Adam watched as a cardinal flitted from one tree to another, a red flash against a gloomy backdrop. The wintry warning of geese could be heard in the distance. Adam stood, ram-rod straight, between Ryan and Jake. The collar of his wool coat scratched the back of his neck, but he ignored the discomfort. Instead, he drew his attention to the small group that had gathered nearby. A baritone voice intoned mournfully, but the wind snatched up the words and hurled them away from Adam.

He hadn't felt comfortable joining the others, so he'd hung back, taking on the role of observer. His eyes remained bone-dry as Justin's polished mahogany casket was lowered into the earth. He could hear Julia and his mother's wails and felt revulsion at their counterfeit tears. How could they love a monster? He felt nothing. He wasn't entirely sure why he'd even come. He certainly would never grieve for the man Justin had become, but he hoped he could someday mourn for the boy he had once been.

Adam turned toward Ryan's car which they'd left parked outside the cemetery gates on the side of the road. He'd wanted to avoid his family as much as possible, so he continued to stay at Ryan's house. He could see the blame in their eyes, hear it in the few words they'd exchanged; it was there--always, like an insidious shadow, so Adam stayed away. Charles had returned from college for the funeral, but Adam avoided him at all costs. As far as Adam was concerned, he was just as bad as Justin.

Adam turned to watch his family members file back into the black limousine. He suddenly realized he felt no ties to them whatsoever. Whatever familial bond was supposed to exist had been severed completely. He felt Ryan and Jake each place a hand on his shoulder, and he knew, without a doubt, that these two friends may not be his biological family, but they were his real brothers.

*   *   *

This had been Ryan's first funeral. He hadn't wanted to come either, but his mother had finally convinced him to be there to support Adam. He felt extremely awkward and was glad when Adam refused to sit with his family by the graveside. He had been there when their son died. Guilt still roiled in his stomach whenever he thought back to that day. If he hadn't had to run back to the car to get his phone, he would have been in time to help Jake pull up Justin. If he'd gone with Jake in the first place, everything could have been avoided.

The "what ifs" plagued him, and his sleep came in spurts, oftentimes interrupted by Justin's final scream. It was that scream that haunted him. It had seemed too long, like he'd fallen forever, but the end was the worst part. It just stopped suddenly, too abruptly, like turning off the TV in the middle of a word—when unadulterated silence is all that is left.

The police questioning had been difficult, and he was glad to have his parents there with him. Two police interrogations within two days—the gravity…it was too much for him and left him utterly drained. The most difficult thing had been talking to Adam afterwards. The police had already given him the bad news, but Adam had wanted to know every detail.

He'll never forget the image of Jake punching Justin over and over. Was that Jake? The guy who always does the *right* thing? The ferocity of the attack froze Ryan momentarily, but profound terror caused him to run faster than he'd ever run before. They were too close to the edge. Ryan had known with complete certainty that death loomed nearby, especially when Justin disappeared over the edge. Ryan witnessed Jake's struggle to keep Justin from falling. He remembered yelling, but all of his movements seemed like slow motion. It was almost like running through knee-deep water.

Then he heard the scream, and he knew. He'd been two seconds too late. He froze in place. It took a moment to find his voice. "Jake?" he'd whispered.

Jake had rolled over onto his back, his eyes glazed over; he was in shock. "My gloves..." he'd muttered, looking at his bare hands.

It took only a moment to realize what had happened. Police later confirmed it once Jake's gloves were found with Justin's body. Justin must have pulled off Jake's gloves, inadvertently causing his own death.

*   *   *

Amber's hair tickled Jake's face, but he didn't dare shift his position. She'd fallen asleep, peacefully curled into his chest. Her deep breaths matched the rocking of Ben Green's favorite overstuffed recliner. The last two weeks had been very eventful. After Justin's death, four girls had come forward to report his rapes to the police. His death gave the girls comfort and a little satisfaction. All the girls had met and started a sort of therapy group. A horrible thing had brought them together, but a friendship based on shared misery had bloomed.

Adam's father had moved to Albany to escape the embarrassment and certain collapse of his law career. He was charged with obstruction of justice, and, if found guilty, would lose his license to practice law. Julia had taken off two days after the funeral like she could smell the prospect of several civil suits and her husband's subsequent financial ruin.

Ryan's parents had invited Adam to live with them so he could finish high school at Brushton-Moira Central. Adam's father was only too willing to agree to the arrangement. Jake smiled as he thought of all the time Adam had been spending with Sandy. "Is he ever going to have the guts to ask me out?" she'd asked Amber and Jake a few days ago. Amber had just laughed, punched Jake's arm, and told her to take matters into her own hands.

Jake lightly caressed Amber's arm, and she murmured sleepily. Her eyelids twitched, and Jake hoped she was having a pleasant dream and not reliving her nightmare. Thankfully, Amber was handling the attack well. Her tight-knit family definitely aided in her recovery process. It had been Amber's idea to form the group comprised of Justin's other victims.

The antique grandfather clock began chiming, and Amber stirred. She sat up and rubbed her eyes. "Sorry," she said sheepishly. "How long was I out?" she asked.

"About a half hour. You missed an entire episode of *The Simpsons*. It was a good one too."

"Why didn't you just wake me up? You must have been bored." She stood and stretched.

"I like it when you sleep. You're just so cute." Jake smiled widely. "Just like a little baby," he added laughing.

Amber jumped into his lap. "Does this feel like a baby?" She began bouncing. "I hope I crush your legs."

"You can't hurt me," Jake teased as he picked her up. He set her gently on the carpet and pinned her shoulders against the floor. "One, two, three," he counted loudly. Jake jumped up and began a celebratory dance. He adopted an announcer's voice. "And still the welterweight champion of the world...Jake Carver."

Patsy walked in the room and Jake blushed in embarrassment. "Honey, what have I told you about letting Jake beat you?"

"You told me to kick his butt and not to let him win," she answered back matter-of-factly. She knew her mother loved to tease Jake as much as she did, so Amber always went along with her. She shielded her mouth with her hand but whispered loudly enough for Jake to hear. "I just don't think he's ready to face these massive muscles." She flexed like a bodybuilder. "Look at these guns, Jake. They are loaded weapons, so don't tick me off."

Jake waved at her dismissively and headed into the kitchen. Amber jumped onto his back. Jake spun around feigning confusion. "Mrs. Green, is there something on my back?" Amber giggled. "I think I feel something, but I'm not sure."

An hour later, Jake was climbing the stairs to his bedroom. His grandparents were already asleep. He turned on the light next to his bed, planning to read a little before he tried to sleep. It was still difficult to turn off his mind at bedtime, and he found that reading about someone else's problems usually took his mind off his own.

When he turned toward his bed, he noticed an envelope propped on his pillow. Nana must have left it there for him. He froze when he saw the return address. It was from Northern State Correctional Facility. His stomach lurched. Did he want to open it? He sank onto his bed and held the offensive object in both of his hands. It was slim, containing no more than one sheet of paper. The handwriting on the envelope was neatly printed. He turned over the envelope and slid his finger inside and tore it open quickly before he could change his mind. He unfolded the white, unlined sheet of paper. It was dated six days ago. The page fluttered in his hands as his fingers shook.

Dear Jake,

    I read an interesting news article the other day while I spent some time in the prison library. Sorry this letter isn't very timely, but it's not like I have access to a computer every day. I digress; however, as I'm sure my complaints will fall on deaf ears. My lack of freedom isn't the topic of this missive; you are, my boy.

I read all about your heroic efforts to save the young man who attempted to rape your girlfriend. How impressive, and, to think, she was being drugged while you were here. Good thing your friends could intervene. It's too bad the poor, disturbed boy fell to his premature demise. I'm sure you hung on like death, though.

I've never been prouder of you, son. You're more like me than I ever imagined. Feel free to visit me whenever you want. Just remember that I know you better than you know yourself.

Love,

Dad

P.S. The gloves were brilliant thinking.

Jake tore the letter to shreds. He was *not* like his father and never would be. Justin deserved to die, and Jake would never regret the decision he'd made. He wasn't sure what had possessed him to toss his gloves over the ledge, but everything had worked out just fine. No one would ever know...the dead keep everyone's secrets.

Made in United States
North Haven, CT
01 December 2023

44861650R00134